MW01105754

GIANT STEPS

Each of us is on a unique journey.
We may not realize it until we reach our destination.

GIANT STEPS

SUFFRAGETTES AND SOLDIERS

MARY BLAIR IMMEL

Giant Steps is made possible through the generous support of Wanda Y. Fortune.

Indiana Historical Society Press | Indianapolis 2017

Printed in the United States of America

This book is a publication of the
Indiana Historical Society Press
Eugene and Marilyn Glick Indiana History Center
450 West Ohio Street
Indianapolis, Indiana 46202-3269 USA
www.indianahistory.org
Telephone orders 1-800-447-1830
Fax orders 1-317-234-0562
Online orders @ http://shop.indianahistory.org

The paper in this publication meets the minimum requirements of American National
Standard for Information Sciences—Permanence of Paper for Printed Library Materials,
ANSI Z39. 48–1984 ∞

Library of Congress Cataloging-in-Publication Data

Names: Immel, Mary Blair, author.
Title: Giant steps : suffragettes and soldiers / Mary Blair Immel.
Description: Indianapolis : Indiana Historical Society Press, 2016. |
Includes bibliographical references and index. | Summary: Bernie and her
  family live in Indiana, where she soon gets involved in the national
  suffragist movement for women's rights.
Identifiers: LCCN 2016043839 (print) | LCCN 2016046138 (ebook) | ISBN
  9780871954077 (cloth : alk. paper) | ISBN 9780871954060 (pbk. : alk.
  paper) | ISBN 9780871954091 (epub)
Subjects: LCSH: Family life—Indiana—Fiction. | CYAC: Suffragists—Fiction.
  | Women's rights—Fiction. | Indiana—History—20th century—Fiction.
Classification: LCC PZ7.I34 Gi 2016 (print) | LCC PZ7.I34 (ebook) | DDC
  [Fic]—dc23
LC record available at https://lccn.loc.gov/2016043839

For Dan, who made my life a wonderful adventure,
and our three sons, Daniel, Michael, and Douglas,
who continue to make my life "interesting."

Contents

Part 3 | 1918 to 1920

PART 1
1916

Prologue

People were always asking Bernie's two older brothers what they planned to be when they grew up.

Nick, the younger of the two, would say proudly, "I'm going to be a soldier just like my Great Uncle Charlie. He fought alongside Indiana's famous general, Lew Wallace, during the Civil War."

"Good for you, young man," people would usually answer.

When people asked her oldest brother, Ben, what he was going to be, he would say thoughtfully, "I'm going to be an explorer and take pictures of strange, faraway places." His hero was John Wesley Powell, the man who led the first expedition through the Grand Canyon.

"An explorer? Well, now, just think of that."

After they posed while Ben snapped their picture with his camera, they would smile and say, "Good for you, young man."

Everyone was pleased about Ben's grandiose plans, except Papa. He would never stand still for such foolishness. "Nobody can make a respectable living as an explorer with a camera." He wanted Ben to become his partner someday at the family store, Epperson's Emporium. Then it would once again become Epperson and Son, just as it had when Papa had first joined his father in the business.

Meanwhile, Bernie waited hopefully for someone to ask her about her future plans. She waited and waited, but no one ever asked her that all-important question. So, Bernie stopped waiting and started piping up to say, "Would you like to know what I'm going to be when I grow up?"

If they paid any attention to her at all, they would smile and pat her on the top of her head. Or, they would say, "I'll bet I can guess."

But Bernie knew they couldn't guess, so she would tell them, "I'm going to be like Nellie Bly."

Usually they would laugh when she said that. Those who didn't laugh would say, in a let's-be-reasonable voice, "A woman's place is in the home."

When she told her Papa about her plans to be another Nellie Bly, he only snorted and asked, "What makes you think you could be a sharpshooter? You have never fired a gun in your life and if you did, you would just fall off your horse."

Bernie sighed and tried to explain: "Nellie Bly was not a sharpshooter. You're mixing her up with Annie Oakley, who rides in Buffalo Bill's 'Wild West Show.' I'm talking about the woman who is a great newspaper reporter. She finds out about things that need to be changed and writes about them."

It didn't take Bernie long to realize that nobody really cared what she wanted to be. In fact, it seemed that nobody thought girls could be anything other than wives and mothers. They simply nodded and said, "Don't worry. Someday you'll meet some nice young man, get married, and raise a family."

Bernie had no objections to being a wife and mother, but she knew there were some other things that she also wanted to do. She decided that she would show them. She was determined that there would come a time when everyone would have to sit up and take notice of her.

1

Wrong Foot Forward

Bernie did not know how long she had been wrapped in the comfortable cocoon of darkness. As it began to fall away, the pale light crept into her consciousness. She was aware that her right arm, throbbing and encased in bandages, was firmly strapped across her chest. Her left arm was stiff at her side and her fingers were clenched into a tight fist.

Bernie pressed her lips firmly together. She lay very still and tried to breathe deeply. "I will not cry. I will not cry." The thirteen-year-old repeated the words over and over inside her aching head. No matter how much her nose itched and her eyes burned, she absolutely would not give in to the desire to let the tears flow. If she cried, then people would know she was awake. It was absolutely vital that everyone think she was sound asleep, especially Mother and Papa. She did not want to have to talk with either of them about the awful thing that had happened.

The other reason Bernie lay so still was because whenever she moved, no matter how slightly, a stab of pain shot through her right arm. Her legs hurt. Her back hurt. She hurt all over from her terrible fall out at the McClarty place yesterday afternoon. The accident had happened so fast that she struggled to remember exactly what had taken place.

* * *

Bernie had known for quite a while that her two older brothers, Ben, seventeen, and Nick, fifteen, were up to something. They had been whispering about it for weeks with Nick's best friend, Jack, who, although a year older than Nick, was in his grade at school. From what she'd overheard and pieced together, she knew they were secretly building a flying machine in the old barn that Mr. McClarty owned. She had even figured out that they planned to test it on the first Saturday after the end of school. They had chosen that day because Papa and Mother were taking the interurban train to Indianapolis. Papa needed to do some business that concerned his store. Mother planned to go along to do some shopping and eat at the fancy L. S. Ayres Tea Room. They would be gone from early morning until late in the evening. The boys were sure that would give them plenty of time to test their flying contraption.

Papa was like most of her friends' fathers—strict. He insisted that his sons do their fair share of work at Epperson's Emporium downtown on the court-house square. Ben worked as a stock boy. Mother and Papa had been happy that he got mostly Bs on his report card the last year. If he continued to earn such good grades his senior year of high school, he would be able to start college at Purdue University the following year. He planned to study chemistry because he thought that would be a help to him with his photography—a lot of chemistry went into developing the film from his camera. He also planned

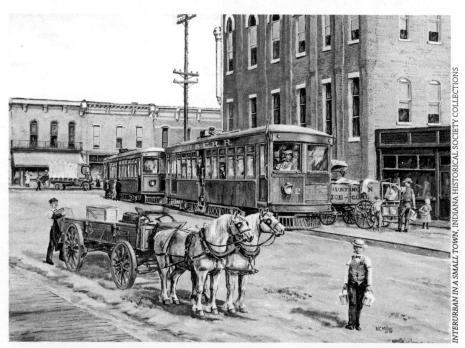

INTERURBAN IN A SMALL TOWN, INDIANA HISTORICAL SOCIETY COLLECTIONS

From 1900 to the mid-1930s interurbans were a popular form of mass transit. The single-car trains were run on tracks that shared the road with horses, pedestrians, and eventually automobiles. Powered by electricity, the cars were tethered to power lines above them. Indianapolis was the central hub for the state of Indiana. Passengers could ride around Indianapolis and to other major cities and towns around the state, such as Lafayette.

on taking geography courses, thinking it would further his plans to become an explorer. Papa insisted that Ben enroll in some business courses as well because he was still determined that Ben would take over the Emporium someday. Ben sighed and agreed to take the courses, but didn't commit to taking over the store. Being the younger brother, Nick had to keep the store swept and clean. However, Papa always gave them the first Saturday of summer vacation to do whatever they wanted. Usually they went to Columbian Park or sometimes they went swimming in the pond out at Mifflin farm where their Aunt Lolly and Uncle Leroy lived.

Jack McClarty's father was even more strict than their own. Papa certainly expected a lot of work from his boys, but Bernie thought old man McClarty was downright mean to Jack. It usually took a lot of ingenuity on Jack's part to get away from work at McClarty's Blacksmith Shop where he did everything from shoe horses to make nails out of iron. McClarty also stabled and sold horses. So, the boys cooked up a plan. The three of them would offer to ride horses out to the McClarty acreage in the country to exercise the animals. The fact that he would be getting work out of someone else's sons, as well as his own, would appeal to McClarty's stingy nature. There were many people who said that McClarty was the most tight-fisted man in Lafayette. Bernie had even asked about it at the dinner table one evening.

Papa looked at her and said, "Mr. McClarty may be a bit . . . well. . . ." Papa seemed at a rare loss for words, but then after careful consideration he said, "There's no denying that McClarty is a sharp man in his business practices, but he's honest. He earns his dollars the hard way. You can trust him to shoe a horse properly. To my knowledge he's never sold anyone a lame horse."

"And," added Nick, "he's downright worried about what's going to happen to his business what with folks riding on the interurban and more people buying automobiles. Horses aren't being used as much as they once were, not even for plowing."

Papa cleared his throat and said, "Now, I think we've spent more than enough time discussing someone else's business at mealtime."

Still, Bernie thought that it was a shame how Mr. McClarty treated his son. Yet, somehow she had never heard Jack say a bad word about his father. Bernie had to admit that he was one of the more agreeable boys she knew. He had always been nice to her. He didn't throw oak apples at her when she trailed after him and her brothers. Sometimes he even tried to get Ben and Nick to let her come along with them. But Jack was usually outvoted when it came to letting Bernie be a part of the boys' escapades, just as he probably would have been outnumbered if he had said it would be all right to let her be a part of what was going to happen on the first Saturday of summer vacation.

So Bernie made her own plans and kept her own secrets. She was good at keeping secrets. She had not confided in anyone, not even her cousin Lizzie, who was also her best friend. Bernie didn't feel guilty about not telling Lizzie. Her cousin would not have wanted to come along anyway. Lizzie preferred more ladylike activities, playing jacks, skipping rope, or making doll clothes. Not Bernie. She wasn't about to be left out of this adventure and let her brothers have all the fun.

She could hardly sleep Friday night, because she was so afraid she wouldn't be ready to follow them. Ben and Nick's upstairs rooms were down the hall from hers at the front of the Eppersons' large two-story house. She opened the windows in her own bedroom as wide as she could, so she would not miss out on the excitement.

When the eastern sky had just begun to lighten Saturday morning, Bernie popped awake at the sound of birds singing—this was what she had been waiting for. Jack was standing in the yard below with the horses. He whistled the secret four-note signal that the boys used. To most people it might sound like a cardinal's call, but Bernie knew exactly what it was and what it meant. Bernie jumped out of bed, pulled on her old brown shoes and laced them up. She had slept dressed and ready-to-go last night. As a matter of fact, she wore Ben's clothes. She had pulled a pair of his baggy overalls on over her skirts. Girls' clothes were such a bother, with bulky skirts always getting in the way. She stuffed them down the pant legs. She wrapped her thick chestnut colored braids around her head and jammed on an old straw hat to cover them. She convinced herself that if anyone saw her they would think she was one of her brothers.

Bernie crept as quietly as she could down the back stairway. She knew her parents were leaving early, and she wanted to be on her way long before they got up. That way she would not have to answer any questions. Mother and Papa would be in such a hurry to leave the house, they would not even notice that none of their children put in an appearance at the breakfast table. If they did notice, they would look at each other in consternation. Papa often commented that it was almost impossible to get children out of bed on a school day morning, but they were up at the crack of dawn on a vacation Saturday.

A bird's-eye view drawing of Lafayette, Indiana, from 1868. The Wabash River is a dominant feature of the landscape, dividing Lafayette and West Lafayette into two separate cities. To the east, the terrain rises, creating many excellent slopes for sledding in winter.

Bernie grabbed the first bicycle at hand, forgetting that Ben's was a bit of a clunker and hard to pedal. Thank goodness their dog Sheppie was nowhere in sight. He had undoubtedly followed the boys. If Sheppie had seen her, he would have given her away with his barking. Even in the early morning, the day was unusually hot for this time in June. She was soon panting, and her forehead was damp with sweat. She was glad when she reached the top of the hill on Union Street and could coast for several blocks.

Bernie rode over the metal bridge across the Wabash River and set off toward River Road. She was making good time when the chain on Ben's bike came off the sprocket. She didn't have time to go back and get Nick's bike. She stopped and managed to get it back on, getting her hands covered with black grease. After wiping her fingers in the weeds at the side of the road, she pedaled away as fast as she could. Her repair didn't last long, though, and she had to stop again. By this time she was hot and upset. What if she didn't get there in time for the test flight? She heard a farm wagon rattling up the road behind

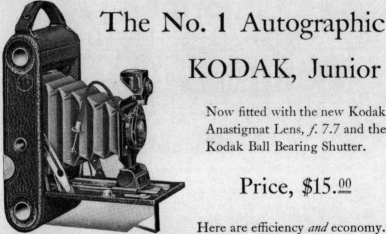
EMERGENCE OF ADVERTISING IN AMERICA DIGITAL COLLECTION · K0207, JOHN W. HARTMAN CENTER FOR SALES, ADVERTISING, AND MARKETING HISTORY, DAVID M. RUBENSTEIN RARE BOOK AND MANUSCRIPT LIBRARY, DUKE UNIVERSITY

*Ben may have used a camera such as this No. 1 Autographic Kodak, Junior. However,
it would have been difficult for him to take pictures that weren't blurry with only one
hand, since one hand was generally used to hold the camera steady at the bottom and
the picture was taken with a lever-like button on top of the lens. This camera allowed
the user to write the date and other information on the negative to record the event and
when the photo was taken. If Ben was taking a lot of pictures at one time he would have
had to stop often to reload film.*

her. She bent over the sprocket, keeping her head down so that whoever was approaching would not recognize her.

"Need some help, sonny?" She recognized old Mr. Granger's voice. Bernie groaned. It would have to be him of all people! He was undoubtedly the nosiest man in town.

Keeping her head down and trying to make her voice sound as deep as she could, Bernie said, "No thank you."

"Is that you, Bernice Epperson?"

She sighed. Her disguise had been a failure. She pulled off the straw hat and let her braids fall below her shoulders.

"Where are you going dressed up like a scarecrow? Is somebody giving a costume party?"

She said, "Not exactly."

"Well, you look right tuckered out. Would you like a ride?"

She hesitated momentarily. She knew Mr. Granger would tell everybody in town he had seen her dressed in boys' clothing. However, she decided to risk it. The broken bicycle and her desire to get to the boys before all the excitement was over, had nearly ruined her plans.

Mr. Granger climbed down from the wagon seat and lifted the bicycle up onto the back of his wagon. This time she wiped her still greasy hands on Ben's overalls and clambered up on the hard wooden seat beside the old man.

"Well now, this is the first day of summer vacation. What will you do today?"

Bernie blurted out, "I'm going . . . I'm going on a picnic."

He turned and looked at her sharply. "Appears like you forgot your lunch."

Bernie sighed, but only said, "Uh-huh."

Fortunately he soon lost interest in the subject and didn't ask her anymore questions. He was too busy telling her about seeing what Henry Schmidt had done that morning. Schmidt had knocked his wife to the ground in their back-yard as she was hanging out the laundry. "That man is going to get his comeup-pance someday because of the terrible way he treats that poor woman." Bernie agreed completely but didn't want to get involved in a conversation about the man whose wife, Edna, helped Mother with their housework. If Papa found out she had gossiped, he wouldn't like it.

Bernie asked Mr. Granger to drop her off at the road that led out to Mc-Clarty's pasture where the barn was located. As soon as Mr. Granger's wagon rattled out of sight, she hid Ben's bike in the bushes. She tried to make her way toward the barn, moving quietly behind a line of sycamore trees. She meant to stay concealed, but it was hard to get a good look at what the boys were doing. She crept closer and closer to where the horses were grazing. She would have been alright if Sheppie hadn't sniffed her out. He came bounding toward her through the undergrowth yipping happily.

"What are you doing here?" Nick, demanded, when he caught sight of her. "And, who else did you tell about this? I suppose Lizzie will be the next one to show up."

Bernie put her hands on her hips and said, "I didn't tell anyone else, especially not Lizzie." Everyone knew that Lizzie simply could not keep a secret.

"How come you always have to hang around us and stick your nose into business that doesn't concern you?"

Bernie had a notion to tell him, but she didn't want to give him the satisfaction of knowing that he, Ben, and Jack were always doing something interesting and exciting. She wanted more than anything to be a part of those things. Boys got to have all the fun.

"Go home," Nick shouted and picked up a dirt clod and flung it in her direction.

As she dodged it, Bernie said, "If I go home, I'll tell—I'll tell what you're up to and someone will come out and put a stop to it." She didn't remember that there wasn't anyone at home to tell.

"Let her stay," Jack said. "Maybe she can help."

Nick turned on his best friend and shouted angrily, "It was you! You told her, didn't you? She would never have found out about this on her own."

Jack didn't answer.

"He didn't have to tell me anything," Bernie said, with her hands on her hips. "I heard you talking and figured it out all by myself."

Ben turned and walked toward the barn, "Forget it, Nick," he said. "We're wasting time. Just ignore her."

It took most of the morning for the three boys to haul their strange contraption up and onto the launching ramp they had built in the barn loft. Ben took photographs of it from every angle. Bernie watched, itching to be part of the action. They could have used her help, as Jack suggested, but every time she stepped forward, Ben and Nick waved her away impatiently. Finally, they got their flying machine into position where they planned to shove it out of the haymow door. By now, the sun was high in the sky, and the boys decided that it would be a good idea to eat lunch before the test flight. They climbed down the ladder and settled in the shade under a large sycamore tree. Bernie found a place to get out of the sun just inside the barn. She sat, gloomily regretting that she hadn't been clever enough to bring a lunch with her. Neither Ben nor Nick offered her anything to eat, and she was determined not to give them the satisfaction of asking for something. They were mistaken if they thought they could starve her out. She intended to stay to the end.

Jack stood up and Bernie heard him say, "I think I left something in the barn."

Bernie sat quietly as she watched him come through the wide doors. He picked up a wooden water bucket and turned it upside down in front of her. On it, he placed half a sandwich and an apple. Then, without a word, he went back outside to join her brothers who were talking and laughing.

She had a mind not to eat any of it, but her empty stomach got the better of her. As soon as he left, she gobbled Jack's offering eagerly. And then an idea popped into her head. She checked to see if her brothers were looking in her direction. When she was satisfied that they were not, she quickly clambered up the ladder and into the loft. She was waiting there when the boys appeared.

The door on the top half of this barn would likely have opened out from a high shelf in the barn where a farmer stored hay. Ben, Jack, and Nick planned to launch their flying machine from such a haymow and out the high door. While it looks like fun, playing in a hayloft such as this could be perilous—as Bernie learned the hard way.

When he saw her, Ben pursed his lips in irritation, but was too busy snapping photos to do anything about it.

Nick, the skinniest of the three boys, climbed onto the seat where the pilot was to sit. Jack grabbed a rope and held on as they tried to control the ungainly craft. He struggled to keep the plane balanced on the sloping boards that were to serve as a runway at the opening of the haymow. As strong as Jack was, he could not hold the weight of the plane with Nick on it.

"Ben," Nick called out. "Take the other rope."

Ben grabbed it with one hand but continued to try and snap pictures with the other.

Ben and Jack were struggling, trying to keep the plane on course as it slid forward.

"Ben, you've got to help us," Nick insisted.

"I can't hold onto the rope," Ben yelled.

"You could if you put the camera down," Nick shouted angrily. "Use both hands."

Ben continued to take pictures. "We've got to record this for history."

Nick shouted, "The right wing is going to hit the. . . ."

"Jump, Nick, jump!" Jack screamed hoarsely as the plane careened forward with a splintering sound.

Bernie rushed forward and grabbed the end of Ben's rope. She tried to hold on, but her feet slipped on the hay in front of the opening of the mow. She felt herself falling. Desperately she tried to hold onto the rope. It eased her fall somewhat, but she hit the ground with a sharp jolt that knocked the breath out of her.

After that Bernie drifted in and out of consciousness, not fully knowing what was happening around her. She didn't feel the rope burns on her hands. She didn't feel the large bump on the back of her head. She didn't know that her right arm was bent awkwardly under her body at an unnatural angle.

Bernie could hear Ben as he bent over her and called her name. It sounded as though he were miles away.

She heard hoof beats thundering on the ground but did not see Jack jump on the bare back of one of the horses. She did not hear him call back as he galloped down the lane, "I'll go get Doc Bender."

Bernie didn't understand when Ben shouted to Nick, "Go tell Aunt Lolly what has happened." She didn't see Nick mount one of the other horses as he rode to their aunt and uncle's farm.

Wilbur Wright flying his glider at Kitty Hawk, North Carolina, in 1901. Gliders, forerunners of airplanes, relied on people launching them and being carried by the wind. Once airborne, the glider could be steered with a controller. This is the type of machine that Ben, Jack, and Nick would have been trying to make and fly.

She was only vaguely aware of the feeling of cool wetness as Ben dipped his red bandanna into the water of the horse trough and bathed her sweaty forehead. She didn't know that her big brother leaned over her to try and shield her from the sun. She didn't understand his frantic words, "Don't die, Bernie." She didn't see that his dirty face was streaked with tears. "Please, don't die, please."

A jumble of strange images flashed in and out of Bernie's semi-conscious awareness during the next several hours. There was pain as the doctor examined her arm. A strange and unpleasant odor filled her nostrils as the doctor clamped the anesthetic mask over her nose and mouth. A loud buzzing sound enveloped her head.

When she awakened, Bernie was in a cool bed. At first, she thought she was at home. It took a while to realize that a woman in a white cap kept asking if she knew where she was.

Then another voice said gently, "You're in the hospital, Bernie." That was Aunt Lolly. "You're going to be all right. Just go back to sleep and rest."

Aunt Lolly was always sympathetic and understanding. She didn't scold before asking how Bernie felt.

When Bernie woke again, she could hear people moving quietly about the room. She could hear whispering. She tried to identify the voices. One was completely unfamiliar—no, it was the nurse in the white cap. Then she heard Aunt Lolly again. Finally, she recognized Papa and Mother speaking softly. Her eyelids were simply too heavy to open and she sank back into a half-awake stage. She could feel someone standing very close to the bed. It was Mother. Bernie did not open her eyes.

"My dear little girl," Mother whispered, as she touched Bernie's forehead gently with her soft hands. "I would give anything to spare you the pain of learning not to reach for things that you cannot have. But, I fear you'll have to learn it for yourself the hard way, just as I did." Mother leaned over and kissed Bernie's cheek. Bernie would not really understand the importance of what Mother had said until much later.

She knew, without opening her eyes that Papa was standing beside Mother. Even though he was whispering, she heard him say, "Whatever will that girl do next?"

Bernie could tell from Papa's tone exactly what the expression on his face must be. His lips would be drawn in a thin line and his nostrils would be slightly flared in exasperation. He would probably be shaking his head in disgust. Goodness knows, Bernie had heard that same question on his lips and seen the irritation on his face many times before.

There had been the day last year when Ben had dared her to climb the big old oak tree in front of their house to rescue a frightened kitten. She had been wearing Ben's trousers then, and her belt had hooked on a branch behind her so that she couldn't get back down. A small crowd of neighbors gathered as the boys went downtown to borrow the tallest ladder from the hardware store. Jack climbed up to get her and the yowling kitten down safely.

Then there had been the time the boys had challenged one of the river gangs to a "battle" in Murdock's Ravine. Bernie had sneaked over and started pelting the "enemy" flank with oak apples. Instead of being grateful for her help, her brothers had turned on her.

Ben had called out, "No girls allowed."

Nick shouted, "Go home and play with your dollies." He lobbed a walnut in her direction. It hit her on the forehead just above her left eye, making a terrible bump. Her eye had turned black and blue.

Jack had rushed forward to stand between her and the barrage, only to be pelted by both sides. He had offered to walk her home, but she shook him off. "Let me alone! I can take care of myself. I don't need a boy's help." She refused to run and stamped deliberately away, her head held high as she endured the catcalls from her brothers as well as the other boys.

No matter what mischief the boys thought up, she seemed to be the one to suffer the consequences. It just wasn't fair. After each incident, Mother would lecture her about unladylike behavior and worry about what the neighbors would think. Papa scolded her about the effect her actions would have on their family's reputation in town. "The Eppersons have been in this place for three generations, and I run a respectable business establishment."

"How come the boys never get scolded?" Bernie demanded of her parents.

Papa sputtered and said, "You don't know what goes on behind closed doors." But she did know. She was certain that Ben and Nick never got the kind of lectures she did. All Papa would usually say to them was, "Try to think about the consequences before you act."

Once in a while Mother would intervene and point out the unfairness of it, but Papa would say, "Boys will be boys, won't they?" It was almost as if he was proud of them and the hijinks that they got up to.

So that was it. It was an unfair world. Boys were allowed to do pretty much what they wanted to do, unless it might get them in trouble with the police. Girls were expected to behave in a different way. Bernie wondered if there would ever come a day when things would change.

2

An Unusual Turn of Events

Papa told Bernie that perhaps her broken arm would keep her from getting into trouble that summer. In one respect he was right, but in another he was quite wrong. It was just the beginning of trouble—or trouble as Papa defined it. For trouble was a matter of one's perspective. Bernie didn't see it that way at all. At first she had thought, as Papa had, that having a broken right arm would limit the things she could do and where she could go. As it turned out, this would be the summer that laid the groundwork for a new direction in Bernie's life.

It started the day her seventeen-year-old cousin, Alice Mifflin, drove up to the Epperson house in the Mifflins' old flivver. Alice had brought her younger sister Lizzie into town to visit with Bernie. Lizzie and Bernie were the same age and in the same classes at school—just like Ben and Alice were. Instead of driving away after Lizzie had settled herself onto the porch swing beside Bernie, Alice got out of the car and came to sit on the front step.

Ben and Nick were busy painting the front porch ceiling and railings. The night before Bernie had heard the boys bargaining with Papa. He agreed that if they completed this chore today, they could have the next day off from working at the store and do whatever they liked. Bernie was frustrated, because it meant that the boys could go off by themselves and there was no way she would be able to tag along. Having her arm in a sling was a great disadvantage.

"It isn't fair," Bernie whined. "How come they get a day off when I don't?"

Nick laughed uproariously, "Why would you get a day off? What work do you do?"

Ben added, "Everyday is a day off for you."

Bernie was dying to know what their plans were, so she settled herself on the porch swing, pretending to drink a glass of lemonade. It was an ideal place for her to listen to the boys' conversation as they painted.

They threatened to splash paint on her if she didn't move, but she stubbornly held her ground. She was certain they were planning another adventure that she would love to be part of, but to her frustration they seemed to be talking in some sort of code that only they understood. Some of the words she heard were "voyageurs" and "archeologists." Was this some new game they were going to play?

When Lizzie and Alice arrived it was impossible for Bernie to pay attention to what the boys were saying, let alone try to figure out what they meant. Lizzie kept chattering on about the party that a schoolmate of theirs was planning and who had been invited.

Bernie could hardly believe her eyes when she saw Alice pick up a paint brush and ask Ben if they wanted help. He looked at Nick and said, "Sure, Carrots, why not? The more help we have, the sooner we can finish this job."

Bernie held her breath, waiting for the explosion. Alice hated it when people called her "Carrots." Alice's reaction to that detested nickname was usually as volatile as her bright red-orange hair. But today, Bernie was surprised that the usual eruption didn't come. Instead, Alice smiled, sweet as sugar, and started to paint.

Just then the hinges on the front screen door screeched, announcing its opening. Mother came out to the porch and said, "I just took some oatmeal raisin cookies out of the oven." She put a platter of them, along with glasses and a pitcher of lemonade, on the small wicker table that stood by the door.

The boys snatched these up immediately.

"Save some for the rest of us," Bernie said.

"Would you girls like to come inside to eat yours?"

Lizzie jumped up and said, "Oh, yes please. I'd like some cookies."

Bernie thought about saying that she didn't want any. Let Lizzie go inside and eat cookies by herself. Bernie would much rather stay outside to watch and listen to the boys, but she took a look at her mother's face. She had seen that *mind your manners* expression before. She sighed and obediently left the porch swing to follow Lizzie inside where they could sit at the large kitchen table at the back of the house. Alice, always the rebel, stayed outside with the boys.

Bernie groaned inwardly when Mother said, "After you girls finish your cookies, you can look through my scrap bag. I'm sure you can find something to use to make doll clothes."

Naturally, Lizzie thought that would be great fun. The afternoon dragged by until Alice finally came upstairs and told Lizzie it was time to go home. Bernie followed her cousins back downstairs. She was disappointed to see that, with Alice's help, the porch painting was completed. Her brothers were nowhere to be seen. Her hopes were dashed. Now she would not be able to find out what they were going to do with their free day tomorrow.

As the three cousins walked out to the Mifflin's auto, Alice asked, "How would you girls like to take a ride with me out to the Wabash River tomorrow?"

"What would we do when we got there?" Lizzie wanted to know.

The Model T Ford had many nicknames, such as flivver, Tin Lizzie, and Leaping Lena. These cars were relatively inexpensive but very durable. Ford Motor Company manufactured more than fifteen million of these cars from 1908 to 1927.

"We could take fishing poles," Alice suggested.

"Not me," Lizzie said, wrinkling her nose. "It's too gruesome to put a worm on the hook." She skipped on ahead and climbed into the car, but Alice hung back and said to Bernie. "We might also spring a trap."

Bernie looked at her older cousin. "What do you mean?"

"You'll see," Alice said with a mischievous twinkle in her blue-gray eyes. "Be ready to leave at eight tomorrow morning. I promise you won't be disappointed. It will be a lot more fun than watching your brothers paint the front porch," she smiled mysteriously.

Bernie persisted, "Do you mean my brothers have asked us to go somewhere with them?"

"Of course they didn't," Alice said. "But I found out where they are going. I also happen to know they are not leaving until nine o'clock. I'll come by and get you. We can be there to surprise them when they arrive."

Bernie's hazel eyes glowed with excitement. How very clever Alice was. She had helped the boys paint in order to learn their plans.

At dinner that night Bernie could hardly contain herself. Unlike her cousin Lizzie, she prided herself on being able to keep a secret, but she was about to burst with this one.

As he passed the meat platter, Papa asked, "Have you boys decided how you are going to spend your day off tomorrow?"

Bernie saw Ben and Nick look at each other like two conspirators. Ben said, "Oh, we'll try to think of something to do."

Bernie didn't dare look at him, but she could not suppress a snicker.

Nick glanced at Bernie and asked, "What are you grinning about? You make me think of a Cheshire cat."

It was all Bernie could do to keep from telling him that she knew exactly what they had planned. Instead she took a bite of green beans and chewed twenty-five times—far more than was needed. With each chew she thought, "Just you wait. Little do you know what's in store for you tomorrow." It was going to be so much fun to beat them at their own game for once.

Bernie was dressed and standing on the front porch eating a piece of bread and homemade grape jam when Alice drove up in front of the Epperson house the next morning. She was surprised to see Lizzie in the flivver.

"I thought you didn't want to go fishing," Bernie said.

"I don't plan to fish, but I do want to go on a treasure hunt."

Bernie looked at Alice. "What does that mean?"

"It means the boys are going out to the old fort."

Bernie loved going to Fort Ouiatenon (wee-ah-tu-non) where a tribe of the Miami Indians had built their village in the early 1700s. She had learned all about it in school. If you were very lucky you could still find relics from that long-ago time when French traders from Canada exchanged glass beads, pottery pipes, colorful blankets, and all sorts of metal trinkets for beaver and other furs trapped by the Indians.

"How did you figure out where they would be?" Bernie asked Alice.

"It wasn't too difficult. They talked a lot while we painted. I kept very quiet, and I think they forgot I was there. Nick mentioned a certain man here in town who often buys historical artifacts. He thought they might earn some money if they could find something to sell to him."

As Bernie settled back on the car seat, she thought how this summer was turning out to be full of unexpected surprises. She had been so sure that her broken arm was going to keep her from doing anything that was fun. Now she was going on an adventure alongside her cousins in the Mifflins' car.

Something was puzzling her, though. Sure Bernie and Lizzie had always been best friends, but why would Alice choose to include the two younger girls—not quite fourteen years old—in her activities?

The day on the banks of the river could not have turned out to be any better. It was bright and sunny. A slight breeze kept it from being uncomfortably warm. Alice parked the car behind a dense clump of bushes where it could not be seen from the road. The three girls spread a blanket and lay on it looking up at a few wispy clouds that lightly inscribed the blue above. Bernie loved the rhythmic sound of the brown river water as it lapped against the muddy bank. She had almost dozed off when she heard the sound of horses' hooves and snorting. The boys had arrived.

The three girls ducked out of sight and waited. They pressed their hands over their mouths to keep their giggles from being heard until Ben let out an indignant shout, "What are you doing out here?"

Nick jumped off his horse and ran over to demand, "How did you find us?"

"As a matter of fact, it was you who found us!" Alice said. "We were here first."

The boys fumed and milled about trying to decide what to do. Finally Nick said, "Well, you can just stay where you are. We'll set up our camp downriver."

While Alice and Bernie fished, Lizzie made wreaths from white catalpa blossoms for their hair. They could hear the shouts from Nick each time he

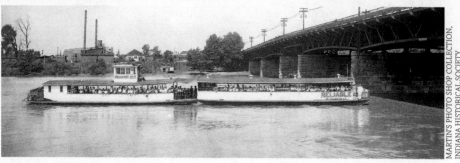

MARTIN'S PHOTO SHOP COLLECTION, INDIANA HISTORICAL SOCIETY

While the Wabash River was a place for a fun afternoon of fishing and swimming, it also provided Lafayette and towns along its banks a way to transport goods. This barge traveled the Wabash River around 1920.

hooked a fish—he was the only one who seemed to be having any luck. Nick posed proudly as Ben took pictures of him holding up his catch.

A little before noon Alice made a great show of going to the car to get a large wicker basket. Bernie had used up all the bait in her bucket and had nothing to show for it, so she was glad to help her cousin. As Alice shook out a large red-and-white checkered tablecloth and lifted the contents out of the basket, she said in a louder-than-necessary voice, "Here girls, have some of this fried chicken. There's enough here to feed an army. Oh, and don't forget the potato salad, Lizzie. I think there are some ham sandwiches, too. I brought a large jug of lemonade and cherry pie for dessert."

It wasn't long before the three boys made their way over to where the food was and began heaping their plates. No one could resist Aunt Lolly's fried chicken and potato salad. Her cherry pie was legendary. No one noticed that the basket contained not just three plates for the girls but enough for all six of them.

After the boys ate, Nick and Jack went out into the meadow to search for treasures. Bernie and Lizzie followed. Nick tried to shoo them away without success. Ben, however, was more interested in taking pictures of the tall sycamore trees lifting their long white arms to embrace the sky. Alice trailed after him.

Bernie felt that she had stepped back in time two hundred years. It was easy for her to imagine that she could smell the smoke from ancient campfires and that the breezes in the tree tops were echoes of voices from the distant past. She could conjure the sound of drums as the Indians signaled the arrival of the French traders in their canoes filled with goods to exchange for furs.

She knelt and with something that was almost reverence, brushed her hand across the blades of grass, longing to find some real trace of those folks from long ago. Bernie wished for something she could hold in her hand and take home with her. She remembered how her teacher had read descriptions to the class from an old book of collected writings by Sandford Cox. He wrote about how his family had been among the pioneers who came into this area back in the late 1820s and how the children of the early settlers thought they had discovered a very rich land because even the grass sprouting in the spring meadow was decorated with colored beads. Those children had not realized that this was where the voyageurs had come each autumn to trade with the Indians.

Over the years, however, the area had been pretty well picked over. It was a rare thing these days to find a relic from those times. Bernie was more than a bit disappointed not to find a single souvenir. She decided that she would have to content herself with only the memory of a pleasant day.

She and her cousins wandered down to the riverbank where the boys were skipping stones. A sudden gust of wind blew Alice's straw sunhat from her head onto the brown water and the current started to carry it away. Jack jumped in with all his clothes on and swam toward it as they all cheered for him. He clambered up the slippery bank with the hat in his hand. It was a soggy mess with the top caved in and the ribbon dripping.

Nick snatched it and plopped it on Alice's head while Ben snapped the shutter on his camera. "That will make a great picture for the school yearbook," he said. Alice laughed as muddy rivulets ran down her face.

As the sun dropped lower in the sky, Bernie realized she would have to go home empty-handed. She hadn't even caught a fish. She picked up her fishing pole and her empty bait bucket and started to put them in Alice's car. Then she noticed her bait bucket wasn't empty after all. At the bottom she saw something that was deep blue. She put the bucket down to examine the object more closely.

It was a bead—a lovely bead the color of cobalt threaded onto a loop of fishing line and lying atop a small nest of green grass. How had it gotten there? She started to call to the others to show them the treasure. It was then that she noticed Jack watching her from a distance. He was grinning in a way that made her feel flustered, and she felt her cheeks burn.

3

Disturbing Secrets

When the girls arrived back at the Epperson home after their day on the Wabash, Bernie said to Alice, "Today was so much fun, until you ruined your hat."

"That old thing was no great loss."

"But it will be so embarrassing—that picture of you with that hat—when it is printed in the school yearbook."

"I don't care. It was worth it," Alice said. "I like being with the boys. It's a nice change from living in a household with all girls."

A disturbing new thought dawned on Bernie. It had been wonderful that her older cousin had come to visit and had taken her and Lizzie to the river. Now Bernie suspected that the reason Alice really came to the house was not to be with her, but to see the boys.

"As a matter of fact," Lizzie said, "She has a crush on Jack. Whenever he can get away from the blacksmith shop, Jack is with Ben and Nick. So if Alice wants to see Jack, she goes where Ben and Nick go."

"Thanks a lot, little sister." Alice reached out and pretended to shake Lizzie gently but ended up by hugging her. "Do you have to tell everything you know?"

"That's how I am," Lizzie said matter-of-factly.

"Indeed I do know how you are," Alice said. "It's my own fault for telling you any of my secrets, but I love you anyway." It was true—even though she was annoying, no one could help loving Lizzie.

"But how could you have a crush on someone like Jack?" Bernie wanted to know.

"Why shouldn't I?" Alice asked.

"Well, he's . . . he's. . . ." Bernie stammered. She couldn't really think of a good reason. "He's different. He's not one of us."

"You mean because he comes from a rough part of town and lives in a run-down house? Is it because he misses school so much because his father makes him work in the blacksmith shop? Is it because he's younger than I am and in a lower grade? Or is it because his clothes are not a nice as the other boys' clothes?"

"Well, I suppose. . . ." Bernie's voice trailed off into nothingness.

"Don't you think that's kind of snobbish?" Alice asked.

Bernie felt angry. "I don't think I'm a snob."

"I didn't say you are a snob. I said that it's a snobbish attitude. You don't think Jack is good enough for us to associate with."

Bernie had never been forced to put her feelings into words, but she had to admit that Alice had voiced exactly what she had been thinking.

Then Alice said, "Your brothers don't seem to feel the way you do. Jack is their best friend. They accept him as he is. He's gentle and kind. He's pleasant to be around."

Jack's father owned a blacksmith shop that may have looked similar to this shop from 1907. Blacksmiths did hard, physical labor in hot conditions. In a shop such as this one, the black-smith used fire to heat iron in order to shape it into tools, repair farm equipment, and in some cases shoe horses. Jack often helped out in the shop rather than attend school. Many teens of this era worked on farms or at other jobs during part of the school year, and many missed school because of the work.

Bernie could not, for the life of her, think of any reason to disagree. In fact, Jack had always been nice to her, and then she remembered the lovely blue bead in her bait bucket. She stood staring at the ground until Lizzie managed to interrupt the embarrassing silence that hung between them.

"Don't worry," Lizzie said, "Alice's crush on Jack won't last long. Mother says Alice is fickle."

"What is fickle?" Bernie wanted to know.

"It means she changes her mind a lot—especially about boys."

Bernie felt irritated that in some strange way a very special day had been spoiled. First she didn't like thinking that Alice only came around because she wanted to be with the boys. She also didn't like that Lizzie could define a word she had never even heard of before today. She never liked it when Lizzie was ahead of her in anything. Now she didn't know which disturbing thought bothered her most.

Bernie was mulling this over when Lizzie continued, "Last summer Alice was sighing over the tennis coach at the park. Before that it was her art teacher. It will be someone else as soon as school starts."

Bernie sighed with relief at that thought. Maybe she could put up with Alice wanting to be with the boys for this one summer, especially if it meant she could enjoy Alice's company. Better yet, Alice could drive her father's automobile and that meant that Bernie could go places that her brothers went. She would not be able to go much of anywhere if it weren't for Alice.

Her older cousin was very smart, too. She seemed to know something about everything. Maybe it was because Alice always had a book tucked under her arm. "I always take a book with me where ever I go," she'd said more than once. "You'd be amazed how much you can read and learn at odd times." With her love of books, it had come as no surprise that Alice had been the top student in the junior class. Like Ben, Alice was planning to go to Purdue, and she wanted to study biology.

Thinking about Alice, Bernie started carrying a book, too. She read at every opportunity. Even Papa, who usually seemed kind of distracted—unless he was scolding her—noticed. One morning at the breakfast table, he looked up at her over the top of his newspaper and asked, "What's that you're doing?"

"I'm reading a book."

"It's not polite to read at the table," Papa said.

"But you're reading," Bernie countered.

"That's different." Papa sputtered. "This is a newspaper."

"But you're still reading at the table."

"Can't a man have a bit of peace and quiet to read his newspaper before going off to work to support his family?"

"If it's okay for you to read the paper, why can't I read a book? Alice says that it's always good to have something to read when you have a spare moment."

"That's a commendable idea," Papa said, folding his newspaper and putting it beside his plate. "I am glad she seems to have more common sense than her father."

Bernie noticed that Mother opened her mouth to say something and then closed it again, choosing to ignore the insult to her brother, Bernie's Uncle Leroy.

"Maybe that girl will be a good influence to help Bernie grow up and not to be so impetuous. Maybe she'll learn to think before she acts," Papa said.

That was what Papa thought about Alice's influence at the beginning of the summer. But by summer's end, he was not so certain about it. He became grumpy whenever Alice came over, mumbling, "Doesn't that girl ever stay home?"

Papa never said such things about Alice's little sister, Lizzie, who had been Bernie's closest companion for years. Most of the time Bernie liked being with Lizzie. Sometimes, though, she got tired of her cousin because it seemed that all Lizzie wanted to do was play with dolls. That was probably because Lizzie had no brothers whose activities seemed a lot more fun than *girl stuff*.

On the other hand, Alice was so much fun to be with. Alice seemed to be everything that Bernie wasn't. Alice was tall like her mother. Bernie was only five foot three inches. Alice was on the girls' basketball team. Alice claimed she joined the team because her father had four daughters and no sons. Lizzie said Alice had joined because the new coach was so handsome.

Everybody, especially Papa, knew how important sons were. A man needed sons to take over his business someday. Of course, Uncle Leroy didn't really have a business—at least he didn't have a big store to run like Papa. Uncle Leroy had a small place downtown on the square where he repaired watches, clocks, and anything else with gears and working parts. However, in spite of the fact that he fixed timepieces, Uncle Leroy didn't keep regular hours like Papa did. He opened his repair shop only when he felt like it. He was considered something of a genius at making mechanical things work. Townsfolk would wait willingly until he opened his doors for business. If they were really

Basketball was created in 1891 and a year later the rules and game were modified for women. The sport quickly became popular among young women in high school and college. Instead of shorts, the girls wore baggy, knee-length pants called bloomers.

desperate, they would go all the way out to the Mifflin farm to take their watch or clock for him to fix. Papa would shake his head in dismay and say, "Just imagine what would happen if I ran my store that way."

Uncle Leroy had inherited the Mifflin farm just as Papa had inherited his store from his father. Unfortunately, Uncle Leroy had no interest in farming. He would much rather be in his barn tinkering with some "crackpot" invention, as Papa referred to them. Papa had no use for such impracticality. Uncle Leroy made a deal with a neighboring farmer to plant the Mifflin fields. When the man harvested them, he and Uncle Leroy split the money paid for the crop.

Aunt Lolly was as unusual as Uncle Leroy. She didn't go to literary gatherings or nice ladylike teas of the kind Mother and Grandmother Epperson attended. Instead, Aunt Lolly belonged to several groups that were busy trying to reform what they considered society's problems. Papa said she was a meddler. Bernie noticed that Mother just clamped her lips tightly closed when Papa ranted about the activities of her brother and his wife.

Bernie saw herself as not at all like her mother. Mother was very proper, while Bernie considered herself to be sort of a tomboy. Of course, she was not an athlete the way Alice was with team sports. Instead, Bernie could climb a tree like a monkey and loved to sit up in the branches where no one could see her. There, in her leafy hideaway, she could observe people coming and going. Her tree climbing had been somewhat curtailed, however, since the humiliation of the "great kitten rescue," as Ben and Nick laughingly referred to it. Bernie also liked to run up and down the hilly area near the ravine, with her hair blowing free rather than in neat braids. Mother and Papa both frowned on that kind of behavior.

"People will think we've raised a young colt and not a young lady," Mother said.

Bernie paid no attention. She risked life and limb—her own and other people's—as she hurtled down Union Street hill on roller skates. Whenever she could persuade the boys to take her along, she liked to swim in the Wabash. She glowed with pride when Jack said she was the best of all of them at rowing a boat and making it go in a straight line instead of zigzagging.

The summer of the broken arm, however, was the summer that Bernie learned to read. It was not that she did not know how to read before that time. She had always devoured books such as *Little Women*, *The Secret Garden*, and *A Girl of the Limberlost*. But this summer she learned from Alice how to read with discernment. Alice told her that to read in this way meant asking questions about what you were reading; she said it was like having a conversation with the author in your head.

"Have you ever asked yourself what you like about the books you choose to read?" Alice had asked.

Bernie didn't have to think for a moment, "I like *Little Women* because I don't have a sister. I think it would be fun to have three of them."

Alice rolled her eyes. "Which of the sisters in the book is your favorite character?"

Bernie didn't have to stop a minute to think before saying, "Jo."

"Of course, she is," Alice agreed. "Jo's everyone's favorite. But why do you like her so much?"

"Jo does things. She's different. She's brave. She gets into trouble sometimes. She wants to do things that people tell her she should not do because she is a girl."

"Right . . . and she opens doors that most people are afraid to open."

Bernie thought about that for a moment to let it sink in. "In the book, *The Secret Garden*, Mary Lennox opened the door to a secret garden and helped a boy get well."

"What about *A Girl of the Limberlost*?" Alice wanted to know.

"Elnora Comstock was different from other girls, too. She didn't fit in and act the way other girls did. She discovered wonderful things about nature and life."

That summer, Bernie began to enjoy books that she would never have been interested in before. Alice loaned her a copy of *Harriet, The Moses of Her People*, a biography of Harriet Tubman, a slave who escaped her master and fled to the North to be free. Tubman had then risked her life by returning to the South time and time again, leading more than three hundred other slaves to freedom.

Bernie also surprised herself by reading the *Daily Courier* every day, just as Papa did. In spite of the fact that Bernie told everyone she wanted to be a journalist like Nellie Bly, she usually only glanced at the newspaper occasionally. Or, she simply scanned the headlines, trying to find an article for a report when her teacher had the class share current events. Now Bernie began reading the paper from the beginning to the last page, where there was a full-page advertisement for Epperson's Emporium that was selling ladies' dresses for $2.50 and mattresses for $10.75.

At first, it wasn't exactly true that she read every page. Bernie skipped the help wanted ads until one day when Alice pointed out that some interesting facts could be found there. "Did you notice that most of the jobs listed for women are for housekeepers and cooks, seamstresses, or people to take care of children?"

Bernie was not the only one who was surprised at her new-found interest in the newspaper. Papa was even more surprised, as well as a bit concerned, when his daughter wanted to discuss some of the articles in the paper with him. She read aloud one article under the headline, "Denver Girls Will Be Taught How to Be Good Wives."

"Listen to this," Bernie read, "All females twelve years of age and older are eligible to take this course. They will be instructed in various household duties and child-raising. Proper respect for husbands will also be an important part of the curriculum." There was another article about how working women were ruining the family. Papa had misgivings about Bernie's growing curiosity.

Bernie noticed that Papa had a strange habit when *he* read the newspaper. He would clear his throat when he found something especially interesting. It was usually something about business or politics. He cleared his throat a lot when he read about what was happening in Europe, something he had been interested in ever since Germany declared war on France two years before in August 1914. He muttered under his breath about "their confounded foreign wars." When he found something that upset him, he would rattle the paper as though he could change the words by shaking them out.

Elizabeth Cady Stanton (1815–1902), seated, and Susan B. Anthony (1820–1906), stand-ing, were early suffragists, who worked for women to have the right to vote. They began work-ing together in 1851. In 1869, they founded the National Woman Suffrage Association.

Bernie learned even more interesting things under Alice's influence. When she was reading a book about women who struggled against injustice, she discovered that the Mifflin girls were all named for famous women. Lizzie was named after Elizabeth Cady Stanton, a woman who spoke out against slavery and who called for women to have the right to vote. Her sister's name, Peggy, was a nickname for Margaret. Peggy was named in honor of Margaret Sanger, who fought for women's rights. The youngest Mifflin sister, Susie, was named for Susan B. Anthony, another woman who fought for women to have the right to vote. The big puzzle was Alice's name. When Bernie asked her about it, Alice smiled and said, "That's for me to know and you to find out."

Bernie asked Lizzie about Alice's name. She was certain to learn the answer since Lizzie simply could not keep a secret. But Lizzie shrugged her shoulders and said, "I don't know. Nobody will tell me either." Bernie made up her mind that she would figure it out if she had to read every biography in the public library.

The summer turned out to be a surprisingly busy one. The girls went on picnics. They played with the new kittens in the Mifflin's barn. In July Alice drove Bernie and Lizzie out to a field where the boys were setting off fireworks. They went to the county fair where Ben got a blue ribbon for a photograph of Sheppie. They went to the carnival when it came to town.

The doctor removed the cast from Bernie's arm in early August. She was shocked to see how withered her arm looked. The puckered skin hung loosely; it was a disgusting grayish color. When that peeled away it revealed pink raw-looking patches of skin underneath.

"You look like a lizard losing its skin," Lizzie said.

The doctor assured Bernie that her skin was normal and she would be just fine. However, he added, "It is possible that your elbow may always be a bit stiff and your arm may never unbend completely. You also might have a bit of discomfort whenever the weather gets cold."

At first, Bernie was very protective of the arm because she was afraid of injuring it again. When Alice invited everyone to the farm for a swim in the pond, Bernie went but did not risk getting into the water. Nick and Ben were splashing and dunking everyone who came near them. She found a log to sit on where she could dabble her feet safely in the cool water. Jack came to sit beside her. "If you want to swim, I'll go with you down to the far end of the pond. I promise I won't let anyone come near you."

"I'm okay, Bernie said. "I don't feel much like swimming."

"Neither do I. We can just sit here together."

Bernie stood up abruptly. "I've got to go now. I forgot that I promised Aunt Lolly I'd help her make the lemonade."

As she walked toward the farmhouse, she thought it was strange that Jack would want to sit on a log with her and talk instead of playing with the boys. Then she remembered that Jack never did seem to like to swim when other people were around. She once asked Nick why Jack always wore a shirt when he did go in the water.

"I guess it's because he doesn't want anyone to see his back."

"Why not?" Bernie wanted to know.

"I suppose it's because of all of his scars," Nick said. Then, suddenly realizing that he'd told her something he shouldn't have, he reached out and grabbed Bernie firmly by both shoulders and glared at her. "Don't you ever dare say a word to anyone about what I told you! Not a word to anyone."

Bernie stared right back at him. "What makes you think I would tell anyone about that?"

She wanted to ask Nick if he had ever seen the scars and knew what had caused them. She thought she could guess. Jack's father always made him work hard and yelled at him a lot. Maybe he was rough on him in other ways.

Indeed, it was a summer for learning new things—surprising new things. It also turned out to be a time for opening unexpected doors. She wondered if this would continue and what those doors might be.

4

Strange Doors Swing Open

One afternoon in early August, Bernie and Lizzie were shopping for school clothes. The heat seemed to shimmer on the sidewalks. The girls' faces glistened with perspiration, and the packages Bernie carried seemed to weigh a ton. They hurried into Graeber's Soda Shop on the corner of the courthouse square. It felt good to put down their shopping bags beneath the wrought iron chairs and rest their hot arms on the cold marble slab of the small round table.

"Do you think your father will let you have that mohair coat you want?" Lizzie asked. "I know it's terribly expensive, but I suppose things like that don't matter if your father owns the store."

"That's not what Papa says. I still have to be careful what I buy," Bernie said. "But I have outgrown last year's coat, so he might let me have it for my birthday later this month."

Bernie ordered her favorite cherry phosphate soda and Lizzie had a sarsaparilla.

"I'd give anything if I could take off my shoes and stockings and walk home in my bare feet," said Bernie.

"You wouldn't dare!" Lizzie's eyes widened with shock.

"No, of course I wouldn't. That would not be a proper thing for a respectable young lady to do, would it? Of course, my brothers can go barefoot and no one says a word. You go barefoot out at the farm."

"Yes, I do, but only out at the farm with just my sisters around."

The screen door hinge squeaked and Alice came in, pulled up a chair next to them, sighed, and plopped a stack of papers on the seat of the extra chair.

"What have you been doing all afternoon?" Bernie asked.

Soda shops, or soda fountains, were places for people of all ages to socialize and enjoy ice cream, malts, shakes, and fountain drinks. Bernie and Lizzie would have enjoyed their sodas at a store much like the one in this 1910 photograph.

"I've been helping Mama get some information sheets put together so we can hand them out at the next meeting of the Lafayette Franchise League." Then she turned to Bernie, "Why don't you come with us to the meeting next Tuesday evening?"

Bernie had never heard the word "franchise." "What in the world is that?" she asked.

Alice replied, "They work for women's suffrage."

Here was another word that Bernie didn't know. "What does that mean? It sounds painful."

"I guess some people would think that word appropriate. The very thought of it seems to bother a lot of men," Alice laughed.

Lizzie piped up and said, "Suffrage has to do with women getting the vote."

"Why don't they just say vote?" Bernie huffed, even more upset that this was yet another word that her cousin Lizzie knew that she did not. "Will the meeting be fun?" Bernie wanted to know.

"That depends upon your definition of fun," Lizzie said.

"I think it's going to be exciting. I can hardly wait," Alice said. "There is going to be a special speaker from England. Here, you can read about her in this issue of our paper." She picked up one of the sheets from the stack on the chair and handed it to Bernie.

Bernie suspected that such a meeting was going to be boring, but she decided to attend anyway. At least it would be something to do, and it was another opportunity to go somewhere with Alice in the automobile. She could usually count on something unusual happening when she was with Alice.

However, on the following Tuesday when she entered the meeting hall, Bernie was disappointed when she looked around. Other than Lizzie, no one else her age was there. She didn't see a person she really knew except the town librarian. Of course Aunt Lolly was there with Alice, but most of the chairs were filled with women she'd never seen. She was surprised to see a few men in the audience, too, but she did not know any of them either.

As Aunt Lolly started to take her seat beside them, she looked up and waved to someone in the far corner of the room. "Oh, look. There's Emily. I'm so glad she has finally decided to come to one of our meetings. You girls stay here. I'm going to sit in the back with her so that she won't feel all alone."

Bernie turned and saw Aunt Lolly headed toward a woman dressed in a shabby black coat. She wore a battered felt hat with stringy ribbons that tied under her chin. Bernie leaned over and whispered in Alice's ear, "Who in the world is that? She doesn't look like the kind of person who would attend a meeting like this."

"She's exactly the kind of woman who should come to a meeting like this." Alice said. Bernie thought there was a bit of a sharp edge to her cousin's words. "Mama has been trying to get her to come for a long time."

"Well, she must feel out of place. Most of the people here are decently dressed. Her hat looks like something taken from a scarecrow. I'm surprised she would have the nerve to wear it out in public."

Alice said, "It is probably the only hat she owns. I'm glad she didn't let false pride keep her from being here tonight. I'm sure it wasn't easy for her to come this evening."

"What do you mean?" Bernie asked.

"I mean that life is very difficult for her. She married when she was quite young. Mama thinks she just wanted an excuse to move out of her father's house. He's a very unpleasant man. Her husband worked on the railroad but was killed in an accident about a year ago, leaving her to care for their two young children. Her oldest child is sickly and can do very little for himself. After her husband died, they had no place to go except back home to live with her father and her younger brother. She does a bit of sewing for people to earn money to help pay doctor bills for her son. Her world might be a lot better if women had the vote."

"How do you know so much about her?" Bernie wanted to know.

"She's a friend of my mother," Alice said, and then added, "I'm surprised you don't know her."

Bernie twisted her head and looked back at the woman again. There was a familiar look about her, but she didn't think she had ever seen her before. "Why should I know her?"

"Her name is Emily McClarty Kennedy. She's Jack's older sister."

Bernie's mouth went bone dry and she felt her face flame red. She sat staring straight ahead, not wanting to see Alice's expression. She desperately wished she had not come to this meeting. After a short while Bernie slumped miserably in her seat, trying to think of a way to escape, but she was trapped with Lizzie on one side of her and Alice on the other. She did not know how she was going to get through this evening.

Bernie did not look up again until she heard a loud rapping of a gavel as the meeting was called to order. "Our speaker has come a long way to be with us this evening. Her name is Isabel Grandison. She is one of a group of women from Great Britain who have been touring our country to tell us what our sisters across the Atlantic are doing for the cause of women's suffrage. We are very fortunate that she was able to speak to us here tonight."

The slender woman who stepped to the speaker's stand was so short that she had to step up on a wooden box so that people could see her. "Thank you Madame President. I am pleased to have the opportunity to be present this evening. I shall begin by saying that one of the things we in England recently have done is to change the name of our cause. We are no longer asking for suffrage. That sounds too pleading. What we want is merely to be accorded our rights as human beings. One of those is the essential right to vote. Out of that power springs all our other rights."

At first Bernie found it difficult to understand not only her accent, but some of the things the woman said. It wasn't long, however, before she heard things that never before had entered her mind. Bernie didn't know that there had been a time when women could not own property in the United States and England. In some places, if a woman's husband died, she had to have a male relative go with her to a court of law in order to get custody of her own children. Women were not allowed to serve on juries in England. Utah, she learned, allowed female jurors in 1898 but very few other states allowed them. Bernie heard how women who worked to support their families worked long hours and were paid low wages. Even little children worked at dangerous jobs in spinning mills six days a week, and many were injured by the dangerous machines. Many young boys worked in coal mines ten-and-a-half hours a day in dark, damp conditions.

Miss Grandison continued, "Sometimes men neglect their families. Sometimes they spend not only what they earn, but even take the pitifully small wages their wives and children bring home. Often the men spend that money on drink at the local pub. That leaves the family without a way to pay rent or buy food."

The young woman's crisp voice continued, "But a change of our organization's name does not imply that we have not suffered. Indeed many of my dear friends who have enlisted in this struggle for their rights have suffered greatly. At first we were merely ignored or simply laughed at when we tried to talk to politicians. We were pushed out of the way and told to go home where we belonged. When we carried banners, people jeered at us. We were called vile names. It did not matter that many of the women marching shoulder-to-shoulder with us came from well-known families. Sometimes stones were thrown at us." The speaker paused momentarily and the faraway look in her eyes told Bernie that the woman was reliving those painful experiences.

The speaker resumed, saying, "We were promised that we would have a hearing in the halls of justice, but we waited in vain. Even the newspapers refused to print our story. We realized then that we would have to resort to more drastic efforts in order to get attention. One of our marchers was accused of spitting in the face of a policeman. It didn't matter that it was untrue. She did not spit, but she was arrested. This brave woman rejoiced because she thought her arrest would put our cause in the public eye. But we still were not given the right to have our case heard in court. Somehow we *had* to make people listen. More of us were arrested. We went on a hunger strike. We refused food. We risked death by starvation. We thought if some of us died it would capture the attention of the people. The authorities could not allow that to happen, so they force-fed us by jamming tubes down our throats. Sometimes the food was shoved down the throat so hard it went into the lungs. That very nearly killed some women."

Bernie marveled that this frail-looking woman and her friends could have endured all the terrible things that had happened to them. She could imagine what a reporter like Nellie Bly would have written about that!

Miss Grandison continued, "And, what was it we wanted? We wanted only the same right to vote that men have taken for granted for generations."

Alice jumped up from her chair, as did many others, and stood applauding as she called out, "Hear! Hear!"

When the applause died down, the speaker said, "Men denied us the vote by using the flimsiest

On July 4, 1917, the National Woman's Party picketed for women's rights in Washington, DC. Helena Hill Weed of Norwalk, Connecticut, was arrested and served a three-day sentence in a DC prison for carrying a banner, stating, "Governments derive their just powers from the consent of the governed."

arguments of all. They claimed they were protecting us. They said women were too pure to be sullied by having to vote. They said that no decent woman had a need to vote. They said we were too emotional to vote."

Miss Grandison closed her speech quietly, stating, "The philosopher and politician John Stuart Mill addressed Parliament in 1867 about getting votes for women. He said that denying women the vote is not only an 'injustice.' It is 'silly.' 'To continue to deny women the right to vote,' he said, 'would mean that women would have to be declared unfit or that their vote would be a public danger.'"

To Bernie's surprise there was no applause following this. There was only silence, as if a prayer had been uttered.

Bernie sat thinking about all the ideas she had just heard. She sensed that she had opened a door and was looking out into another world. Her own problems suddenly seemed to shrink in importance. She didn't like it that her brothers could do things that she was not allowed to do simply because she was a girl. However, Bernie now realized there were things going on in the world that were far worse than the trivial things she complained about. There were brave women who risked their lives trying to do something about greater injustices. Yes, Bernie knew she had opened a door, but was she ready to step through it? That would be a giant step.

After Miss Grandison's speech, Bernie heard little of what was going on around her until the president of the group rapped her gavel loudly to make an announcement: "Miss Grandison has given us much to think about. We could have had no better inspiration than she has been as we start making plans for this year's annual Lafayette Franchise League Essay Contest."

At the words "essay contest," Bernie started to pay attention.

"These essays are to be no more than one thousand words in length. This year's theme is 'Why the world will be a better place when women get the vote.' The winning essay will be published in the *Daily Courier*. The deadline for entries is November 30. The winner will be announced on the first day of January 1917, and her essay will be published in the paper that month. What better way for us to start a new year of our work for women's rights?"

Bernie glanced at Alice, who whispered to her, "You want to be a reporter. Here's your chance to get published in the newspaper."

Bernie decided this would be easy as pie. She always got good grades on her essays in school. She could probably do it in a couple of evenings. Papa would see that she was putting her time to good advantage. He might be proud of her, especially if her piece was published in the newspaper. When she got home that evening, Bernie started to write her essay.

5

The Rocky Road to Fame

Bernie couldn't forget about the things she had heard at the suffrage meeting, especially the theme of the essay contest. The next evening at the dinner table, just after the pot roast had been passed around, Bernie turned to her mother and asked, "Do you think the world would be a better place if women could vote?"

Mother looked startled and dabbed at her lips with her napkin. She opened her mouth but no words came out. However, she didn't have to come up with an answer because Papa stared at Bernie and asked, "Why in the world would you ask your mother such a strange question?"

Bernie said, "I just wondered. There are people who think that women will get the vote someday."

Papa said, "There is no need for Mother to vote. Why would your mother want to vote? In fact, why would any woman want to vote?"

Bernie said, "Maybe Mother has some ideas of her own. Maybe there are some things that Mother would vote to change." Once again Mother dabbed daintily at her mouth with her napkin and looked at Papa. Papa just looked irritated. Bernie knew she was on thin ice, but she persisted.

"Would you vote for a candidate who promised to end child labor?"

"I'd vote for that," piped up Nick, who had been scolded that afternoon for not filling the wood box next to the kitchen stove.

"I'll second that," Ben chimed in, "Then I wouldn't have to unpack all those boxes at the store."

"Or stack cans on the shelf," Nick added. "Or sweep the store every evening."

"Down with child labor," Ben chanted.

"Oh, do be quiet," Bernie said. "This is a serious matter."

"I'm deadly serious," Nick said. "Besides, I don't know why you care about child labor. I don't see you doing any work."

"That's all you know. Mother sends me upstairs to look under your bed when it is time to get the laundry ready. I have to pick up your dirty, stinky socks," said Bernie. "Besides that's not the kind of child labor I'm talking about. I'm talking about little children working in mills or mines." She turned toward Mother and asked, "Do you think little children should be doing such dangerous jobs? Would you vote for a candidate who promised to end that kind of child labor?"

Mother seemed flustered. "Well, I suppose I never gave it much thought."

Bernie could not let the argument go. "And what about women who work for a pittance at terrible jobs? Or how about the men who take their wives' hard-earned money and waste it in saloons when their own children need food?"

"I'm sure I wouldn't know about such things," Mother said.

"Exactly right," Papa said. "Decent women like your mother shouldn't have to be bothered with that kind of unpleasantness. Politics is a dirty business. It's a man's business."

"Yes, it certainly is dirty business—because men have been running things for so long."

"It comes down to this," Papa said in a tone that made clear he expected to be listened to. "I'm sure your mother knows that I am looking out for her best interests. I see to it that she has a comfortable life. In fact, I believe it is my responsibility to make certain that all of you have everything you need."

"But Papa, there are many women who do have to work in order to feed their children. If women could vote, maybe things would change. Don't we care about them? Or do we care only about ourselves?"

"Be careful, young lady," Papa said. "You are on the verge of being impertinent."

"I don't mean to be rude," Bernie insisted. "I just want to know how Mother feels about such things. Surely she has a right to her own opinions."

"Eat your dinner and do not bother your mother with such drivel," Papa said.

Bernie could not let the subject alone, even though it was clear that Papa felt the matter was settled once and for all. "What about women who don't have anyone to look out for their best interests? What about women whose husbands don't take good care of them?"

Papa said, "I think we have talked enough about this subject. Women will never have the vote." With that, he finally lifted his fork to his mouth. The table

As Bernie discovered, young children were working difficult and dangerous jobs in factories and mines around the United States. In many cases, these children received little or no schooling because they worked long days. They also received very little pay. These photographs, taken by Lewis Hine in 1908 for the National Child Labor Committee, are of children working in factories in Indiana. The girl above is making a melon basket in a basket factory in Evansville. The boys are working in a cigar factory in Indianapolis.

FRANK LESLIE'S
ILLUSTRATED
NEWSPAPER

No. 1,732.—Vol. LXVII.] NEW YORK—FOR THE WEEK ENDING NOVEMBER 24, 1888. [Price, 10 Cents.

WOMAN SUFFRAGE IN WYOMING TERRITORY—SCENE AT THE POLLS IN CHEYENNE.

In 1869 Wyoming was the first territory in the United States to grant women the right to vote. Despite the U.S. Congress's strong opposition to granting Wyoming statehood as long as women had this right, the residents refused to give up women's suffrage. The women in this image from an 1888 newspaper are lined up to cast their votes in this northwestern territory. Two years later President Benjamin Harrison of Indiana granted Wyoming statehood, making it the first state to have women's suffrage as a legal right.

was quiet for a few moments with only the clinking of forks and knives sounding against china plates.

Bernie put down her fork and said, "Did you know that women in Wyoming were able to vote as early as 1869? In fact, when our own President Benjamin Harrison signed their statehood bill, he called Wyoming the 'Equality State.' That was because when they entered the Union, they declared they would not do so unless women could vote."

"Where did you hear such balderdash?" Papa demanded.

"I'll bet I know where she got it," Nick piped up. "She got it from Alice. Alice is always filling her head with a bunch of stupid ideas like that."

"It is not stupid," Bernie said. "It happens to be true."

"Oh, yeah?" Ben said. "What do you know about Wyoming? Have you ever been there?"

Bernie started to admit that she had, indeed, gotten the information from one of the papers Alice had given her. Then she thought better of it. "I don't have to go to Wyoming to know about that. I read it in the newspaper," Bernie countered. She didn't add that the newspaper was one of the women's suffrage publications. "Well, everything you read in the newspaper isn't true," Ben said.

Papa brought his fist down so hard on the dining room table that the china cups rattled in their saucers. "Enough of this. I would like to be able to eat my evening meal in peace." Papa's face was very red.

Bernie glanced at Ben and Nick. They looked as startled as she felt. They seldom saw Papa get as upset as he seemed to be tonight. She looked at Mother to see what her reaction had been. Mother held her napkin up to her mouth. Bernie couldn't be certain, but she thought she had glimpsed a slight smile on her mother's lips.

"There will be no more conversation at this table unless it is civilized," Papa said.

"And I suppose this is how civilized men settle an issue," Bernie mumbled under her breath, "by pounding on the table and refusing to talk about it."

"What did you say?" Papa demanded.

Bernie shook her head. "Nothing, Papa."

That evening, Bernie went up to her room and went back to work on her essay. She soon learned it wasn't going to be as easy as she had originally thought.

* * *

It took Bernie a few weeks instead of just a couple of evenings to complete her essay. It also took enough sheets of crumpled paper to fill her wastebasket twice over. She wrote it and revised it. She could not believe how difficult it was to say all that she thought needed to be said in just one thousand words. Before she made a final copy, she looked up the definition of a few words and checked the spelling of others. She painstakingly copied her essay until it was perfect, even though it took several tries to get pages without any ink blots on them. When she was satisfied that it was the best she could do, she looked at it with satisfaction. She wondered what Alice would have to say about it. It seemed important to get her approval. That night she tucked it carefully into her book bag.

Bernie could hardly wait until school was over the next day. She met Alice as she was coming out of her last class and handed her essay to her cousin. Alice sat on the top step outside their school to read it. Bernie watched expectantly, but Alice continued to sit silently. She read it through once, and then she read it again.

Bernie looked at her and asked, "Well, what do you think?"

"I'm sure it would get an excellent mark in English class. There are no misspelled words. You used good grammar. Your sentences are complete. You have even included some quotations from famous people, but. . . ."

"But, what?" Bernie wanted to know.

"It's. . . ." Alice pursed her lips and paused a long time. Bernie knew Alice was trying to find the right words."

"You think it's . . .boring?" Bernie said.

"I didn't say it was boring. Boring is not the word for it," Alice said, and sighed. "In fact, it's perfect." Bernie started to smile but stopped when Alice said, "Yes, it's perfect. Too perfect. There's just no heart in it. You are holding the subject at arm's length. I don't get the feeling that you really care about suffrage or believe in your words. Anyone could have written this. It's not very original. You just strung together things that other people have already written or said."

"But I put in all the facts. I wrote how Abigail Adams told her husband, John, to remember the ladies when the men wrote the Constitution. I wrote about the early American poet, Anne Bradstreet, and the colonial religious leader Anne Hutchison, great women who would not be silenced. I even used some of the things that Miss Grandison talked about in her speech."

"Indeed, you did all of that," Alice said. "But you asked me for my opinion. I thought you were serious about your writing, so I did you the favor of telling you how I really feel."

Bernie snatched her essay out of Alice's hand. "Just forget about it. I don't want to enter the silly old contest anyway."

Bernie huffed and stamped down the stairway. She didn't know whether she was more hurt or angry. She stopped in front of the large trash container by the door and ripped the pages of her essay in tiny pieces and let them flutter into it, along with her bitter tears.

6

Secrets and Scary Business

Bernie could not believe her eyes when she looked from her bedroom window to see who or what was causing such a racket in front of her house. A horn blasted repeatedly. Sheppie added to the uproar by barking loudly as he charged out of the house across the front lawn out to the car and back again. Papa sat in the Hupmobile, his new touring car. He had the top down, and he wore a plaid sporting cap that she had never seen before. Bernie shook her head in disbelief. This wasn't at all like Papa. What in the world had gotten into him?

"For goodness sake," Mother called. "Everyone hurry and get into 'that machine,'" as she called it. "Get in before the neighbors send for the police and we all end up in jail for disturbing the peace."

Bernie was still trying to tie the bow on her middy blouse as Mother thrust a large bowl of potato salad into her hands. The boys came clattering down the stairs behind her. Mother immediately loaded their arms with more dishes of food.

"I don't want anyone to leave this house without carrying something," she commanded.

Sheppie raced around them in dizzying circles as they trooped outside to where Papa waited, still honking. The dog nearly knocked Mother to the ground as she tried to climb into the front seat balancing the large basket she carried. She shoved the dog out of her way, but he managed to clamber into the back seat where he sat panting happily between Nick and Ben.

"Get that creature out of there," she ordered. "He'll slobber all over the food. Bernie, get up here in front with me. I don't want you to drop the potato salad."

Papa, who was usually a model of decorum, continued to honk the horn as they drove away from the house. He waved heartily and tooted at everyone he saw.

Bernie whispered to Mother, "What's wrong with Papa?"

"It's this new automobile," she said. "There seems to be something about these machines that cause men to behave in a most peculiar manner."

Bernie was flung against her mother as Papa swerved onto River Road. "Do slow down before we spill the food," Mother insisted, as she and Bernie clutched frantically at the things they held in their laps.

Bernie felt a bit giddy herself, but it wasn't Papa's new car that made her feel this way. It was the crisp fall air. It always revived her after the final blast of late September heat had sucked away most of her energy.

Today was Aunt Lolly's birthday and they were going to a family potluck dinner out at the old Mifflin farm. It was the home place where Mother and Uncle Leroy had grown up.

Bernie could hardly wait to see the farm up ahead. She loved coming out here. She thought that it must be her favorite place in the entire world. The old house never looked more festive than it did today. Bright orange pumpkins perched in a line on the railings of the wrap-around porch. Dried corn shocks were tied to every post. A large bittersweet wreath with clusters of rust-colored berries hung on the front door. There were baskets of red and green apples beside the kitchen door. She knew there would be a large kettle of hot spiced cider simmering inside. She saw piles of russet, scarlet, and golden leaves raked up in the yard for burning later on. She loved to inhale their fragrance. It was like some exotic tea on sale at Papa's store.

It was always a treat to be at the farm in autumn, although she loved every other season out here as well. In fact, she never could decide which time of year was her favorite. In winter she could hardly wait until the pond froze over so they could go ice skating or ride in the sleigh. But, as much as Bernie loved winter at the farm, she was glad when springtime finally burst upon them in a cloud of white dogwood blossoms and they could hunt for mushrooms in the woods. When Bernie and her brothers were small, Grandpa Mifflin had made a swing to hang from the limb of a gnarled old burr oak tree. Both the tree and the swing were still there, although the wooden seat and frayed ropes had been replaced many times. In summer, the cousins gathered as often as they could to swim in the pond on hot, sticky summer days. Bernie still squealed when tiny minnows brushed against her legs in the dark water.

Hupmobile sedan model N, ca. 1916

Bernie also liked to help around the farm. She remembered going with Grandma Mifflin to gather eggs, even though Bernie had to summon all of her courage to stick her hand beneath a sitting hen. She did not like those menacing beaks.

"Just stick your hand right under her and take the eggs," Grandma instructed.

Bernie looked warily at the vein on the back of her hand. "But what if she pecks me, and I bleed to death?"

"Well, I expect you would get your name in the newspaper. Of course, I don't think I ever heard of anybody bleeding to death from a hen peck." Grandma Mifflin was the exact opposite of Bernie's very proper Grandmother Epperson. Grandma Mifflin could make everything fun, even gathering eggs. Bernie simply could not imagine Grandmother Epperson in a henhouse.

As Papa drove down the long lane and parked the car, Bernie saw the screen door to the kitchen closing behind a familiar figure.

"How come Jack McClarty is here?" she said. "I thought this was supposed to be a family party."

"Well, it is Aunt Lolly's birthday party and it is at her house. I suppose she can invite anyone she wants," Nick said.

Papa added, "Well, everybody knows how your Aunt Lolly is. She never turns any stray animal away from her door."

Papa's words hovered like a storm cloud in the air. She wondered if he realized how unfeeling his words sounded. It was that same humiliating feeling that had engulfed her at the Lafayette Franchise League meeting when she had made the comment about the hat Jack's sister had worn. Now she was embarrassed both for herself and for Papa.

Bernie knew she ought to say something, but she could not form any words to make things right. The glorious autumn day seemed tarnished. She wished with all her heart that she had not mentioned anything about Jack being here for the party. Would she ever learn to think before she spoke?

* * *

As Bernie entered the kitchen, she heard Jack saying to Aunt Lolly, "My sister said to be sure to thank you for inviting her and the children to come to the party, but Georgie was not feeling well enough to come."

"I wish they could have been here," Aunt Lolly said, giving Jack a motherly hug. "Now, you be sure to remind me before you leave to send some birthday cake home for them."

Even though he had said it badly, Papa was right. Aunt Lolly did have a reputation for never turning anyone away. Bernie felt a rush of emotion sweep over her. She threw both arms around her aunt. "I'm so proud I have you for my aunt." She wiped stray tears from her eyes.

Aunt Lolly seemed surprised at Bernie's sudden outburst but countered with a hug of her own. "Well, I am proud to have you for my niece."

Mother came in, followed by the boys. "Lolly, you shouldn't be in the kitchen today of all days. It's your birthday. You ought to sit and let us do the work."

"Oh, you know me; I'm never happy unless I have something to do to keep me busy."

After dinner had been eaten and the dishes washed up, Papa didn't even fuss when Uncle Leroy dragged him out to the barn to see his latest invention. Bernie suspected that Papa would see this as an opportunity to show off his new automobile as they crossed the yard. Mother and Aunt Lolly lingered at the kitchen table, visiting over steaming hot cups of tea.

The boys started to sneak out the back door, but Alice caught them. "Oh, no you don't. Everybody, come into the parlor."

They let out a groan in unison. Nick said, "It's not your birthday. We don't have to do what you say."

"I have a new game," Alice announced. "We need everyone to play it."

There were more groans from the boys, but Bernie noticed that they turned toward the parlor. Not for the first time, Bernie wondered what it was about her cousin that gave her the ability to get people to do what she wanted.

The younger girls, Peggy and Susie, begged to be allowed to play the game with the older cousins. Motherly Lizzie, who treated her younger sisters as though they were her beloved dolls, pleaded their case. It was clear that Alice had not counted on this turn of events but she gave in with a pained smile.

The game was called "Truth or Dare." Each person was handed eight slips of paper. Alice instructed them to write down one question on each piece.

"Should they be arithmetic problems or history questions?" ten-year-old Peggy wanted to know.

Alice started to explain, "They should be questions that make you. . . ."

"She means stuff that embarrasses you," Nick interrupted. "Questions that nobody wants to answer. Questions like: 'What's your secret ambition?' or 'What scares you the most?' or 'Have you ever cheated in school?'"

"I'll help you," Lizzie offered as she sat down beside Peggy.

After much pencil-gnawing and giggling, each paper was folded and put into an old felt hat, which Alice had dragged from the closet beneath the front stairs.

"Hey, why don't you use your beautiful hat that got dunked in the river this summer?" Ben wanted to know.

Alice ignored him as she continued to describe the game. "Each person has to take a turn drawing one of the folded papers from the hat."

"Let me go first," eight-year-old Susie insisted. Before anyone could stop her, she reached into the hat and stirred the papers.

"Just pick one," Lizzie instructed.

Little Susie read her question aloud, "Who have you kissed?"

Bernie glanced at Alice. Alice had probably written that question. She was even more certain that her cousin had not intended for her youngest sister to get it.

"You don't have to answer that," Alice said and tried to remove it from Susie's hand. "Let's pick another one that suits you better."

Nick, who was sat between Jack and Ben, nudged them with his elbows and grinned broadly.

"I like this question just fine," Susie said. "I want to answer it."

Alice sighed as Susie replied happily, "I kiss Calico all the time."

"Calico is a cat, not a person," Lizzie said.

"Well, I kiss Mama and Father, too," Susie said, while everyone roared with laughter. "What's wrong with that?" the little girl asked. "They are persons, aren't they?"

"It's okay, Susie," Jack said, "That was a fine answer."

Alice said, "Okay, Susie, put the slip of paper back into the hat and choose someone to be next."

Again Susie took a long time to make her choice. She walked around the circle three times. Twice she started to offer the hat to someone but snatched it back.

"Try to make your choice before midnight," Ben said.

"Right. You've only got four more hours," Nick added.

Finally, Susie held out the hat to Lizzie, who stuck her hand into it and pulled out a tightly folded paper. She pursed her lips and then read it aloud. "Tell your most closely guarded secret."

Everyone laughed loudly. Lizzie stared at them. "What's so funny about that?"

Bernie said, "It's funny because we all know you don't have any closely guarded secrets. You always tell everything you know to everybody."

"Oh, well, then you will be surprised to know that I am going to enter a very important contest. If I win, it will get published in the newspaper. Furthermore, my English teacher said that if I win that contest, she'll give me extra credit. Then I'll be sure to get an 'A' in the class."

No one seemed especially interested in Lizzie's deepest secret—except Bernie. She felt the hair on the back of her neck rise in hackles. Lizzie had to be talking about the Lafayette Franchise League Essay Contest. Furthermore, Lizzie had persuaded their teacher to give her extra credit. That meant Bernie would have to work that much harder to get the top grade in their English class that semester. She simply could not bear the thought of Lizzie getting ahead of her. She wished now that she had not torn up her essay when she had decided not to enter the contest.

Bernie saw Alice glance at her. She could guess what her older cousin was thinking. She had read Bernie's essay and found it wanting. With her big sister's advice, Lizzie had a very good chance of winning. There was no way Bernie could ask for Alice's help now.

"Okay, Lizzie, it's your turn to choose somebody," Alice said.

Lizzie went over to Jack. He seemed reluctant to play, but he finally drew a truth or dare slip from the hat and read it. He laughed when he read it aloud. "What is your worst subject in school?"

"That's easy," he said. "Almost every subject I take is my worst."

Everyone groaned. Ben said, "That's not fair. Too easy. Who put that one in?"

Jack quickly passed the hat to Bernie.

Bernie closed her eyes and selected a tightly folded piece of paper.

"Read it aloud," Alice said.

"What was your most embarrassing moment?" Bernie paused just long enough for Nick to shout out, "How about the time you baked cookies for Mother's tea party and used salt instead of sugar?"

Ben said, "If she had let us taste the dough like we wanted to, we could have told her how bad they were. But I think her most embarrassing moment was the time she dropped the offering plate in church and the coins rolled around under the pews. It made a terrible racket on the wooden floor."

"Wasn't it right after that the church ladies had a fundraising drive to buy carpeting for the church?" Nick asked.

Lizzie seemed to be enjoying this and added, "Or, the time in school when you didn't know Miss Pringle was standing right behind you and you. . . ."

"I thought this was supposed to be *my* question," Bernie cut in. "But since you've all answered it for me, I guess I don't have to."

"If you don't answer, you have to take the dare," Ben insisted.

Bernie stood up, hands on her hips. "Okay, I'll take your dare," she said defiantly. She would show the boys she could handle anything they could dish out.

Ben and Nick looked at each other. They whispered briefly before Nick announced, "We dare you to walk all the way around the pond by yourself."

By this time, it was as dark as a cavern outside. The boys knew full well how frightened she was of the dark. Nevertheless, she would do anything to get out of this room where everyone was laughing at her expense.

Ben said, "She'll never do it. She's a scaredy cat."

"What is there for her to be afraid of? Any smart wolves would probably run in the opposite direction if they knew her as well as we do," Nick added.

Bernie glared at him. "Okay. I'll do it. I'll show you."

"Take a flashlight," Alice said. "So, you can see and not fall in a hole or trip over a log."

"Yeah, and that way we can watch the light and make sure you really go all the way around," Nick said.

Bernie squared her shoulders and marched from the room and out the front door. As she trudged past the barn, she wished she hadn't been so brash. By now the air had turned cold. She was glad she had worn her new mohair coat to keep warm. But nothing could shield her against her fear of the darkness she was entering. She didn't dare turn back, though. She would never hear the end of it if she did. A screech owl's unsettling cry made her scalp tingle. She shivered at the sound of small animals scurrying through the stubble at the edge of the field.

Bernie's heart thudded inside her chest as she got farther from the farmhouse. She paused for a moment until she heard Nick's taunting voice call out, "We can see where you are. What are you waiting for? Keep going."

Bernie sucked in a deep breath and gripped the flashlight in her hand. It was as much a weapon as a beacon. She started into the small grove of scrub cedar near the shoreline and tried not to pay any attention to the strange noises in the bushes. It was probably just rabbits or raccoons. She heard a shrill howl. She heard wild yipping and hooting. She knew that it was probably Ben and Nick trying to scare her.

As she moved deeper into the woods, Bernie kept reminding herself that she had walked around this pond dozens of times before. But those walks had always been in daylight. Things always looked different and more frightening at night.

Even with the flashlight, Bernie couldn't really see anything. She stumbled over a root and fell to her knees, dropping the light, which rolled just beyond her reach. She tried to stretch out and grab it, but she could not move. She was held back by a thorny bush that clawed at her, scratching her hands. As she struggled to free herself, Bernie heard the sound of fabric ripping. She started to cry softly. This was the expensive new coat she had coaxed Papa to buy for her.

When Bernie heard a crackling noise, she held her breath. Something was moving through the undergrowth in her direction. The sound came closer. She expected to see the yellow eyes of a wild animal glowing in the darkness. She

Although a farm pond can be a fun place to play during the day, at night it can be a treacherous place to walk, as Bernie discovered.

began to whimper softly. Suddenly Bernie felt a hand on her shoulder; another hand clamped firmly over her mouth.

"Don't scream," a voice said in a breathy whisper that made her inhale sharply.

She tried to cry out, but the rough skin of the hand was still pressed tightly over her mouth. She managed to force her lips apart enough to bite the fingers. She heard a gasp of pain as the hand released.

"Why did you bite me?" It was Jack.

"What are you doing here?" she asked.

"I followed you so that you wouldn't be afraid in the dark."

"Is that so? Well, you managed to scare me nearly to death sneaking up on me."

"I'm sorry," he said as he picked up her flashlight.

Bernie would not have admitted for the world how relieved she was to have him here. Instead, she snapped, "The dare was for me to walk around the pond by myself and that is what I fully intend to do. I'll show them that I am as brave as any boy."

For the first time she could remember, Jack seemed irritated with her. "Look, you don't have to prove anything to me. I don't care if you wish you were a boy instead of a girl."

"Being a boy is the last thing in the world that I would wish to be," Bernie insisted. "What I really wish is that people would quit telling me that I can't do things just because I happen to be a girl. Now, let me get on with it."

He turned the flashlight on her.

"You are not going to get on with anything without some help. Now be still while I get your coat untangled from these brambles so you can stand up."

"Be careful that you don't tear my coat anymore than it already is," she ordered. She immediately felt ashamed by her tone of voice. She felt a sharp rock pressing painfully into one of her knees. She groaned as she tried to shift her weight without tearing the coat.

Jack asked, "Are you okay?"

The rock and the cold ground made her miserable. She tried to move her knees, but could not.

"Lean against me," Jack said.

She put one arm on his back and leaned heavily on it. He gave a muffled yelp. She remembered last summer when she wondered why Jack never took off his shirt to go swimming. From what Nick had told her, she imagined that Jack's father might whip his son as hard as he whipped his horses.

"I'm sorry if I hurt you," she said, then added lamely, "I guess my elbows are sharp."

It seemed to take forever until Jack worked the coat free. He helped her get to her feet. She had been kneeling so long that her legs were shaking. She felt his strong arms steadying her until she got her balance once more.

"Thank you," she said, her voice not sounding very grateful even in her own ears.

He leaned closer and said, "I'm glad I could help."

She was too startled to say anything and moved quickly away from him. She was very much aware that he trailed closely behind her as she finally completed circling the pond.

When they reached the barn, he said, "Nobody needs to know I was out here."

"I'm glad you rescued me," she said in a meek voice. It didn't sound like her voice at all.

Bernie breathed a sigh of relief when she reached the clearing and found the path that led up to the house. She stayed outside on the porch for a few minutes while she tried to think what she would say when she went inside. Bernie paused in the front hallway to take off her coat. She was relieved to see that the tear wasn't as serious as she imagined. Probably Edna Schmidt could mend it so Papa would never have to know about it.

Bernie brushed herself off and smoothed her hair. Then she tightened her lips into a determined line. If anyone made any remarks, she would face them down. She had walked around the pond. She had not asked Jack to follow her. But when she went inside, no one said a word. They were all too busy eating freshly popped corn from large bowls. She was surprised to see that Jack had somehow managed to sneak in the back door. He was sitting in the parlor with the others, acting as though he had been there the entire time.

Ben looked up and said to Bernie, "Well, you certainly took long enough." He glanced at Jack and smiled. Jack looked away. To her relief neither Ben nor Nick said anything else.

Back home that night, Bernie got wearily into bed. What a strange day it had been. She wished she hadn't been so unpleasant to Jack when he followed her. She had to admit that she could not have gotten her coat unsnagged from the thorns without Jack's help. She remembered the way he had cried out when she leaned on his back. His arms had been so strong when he lifted her up from the ground and steadied her. Alice had been right when she said Jack was thoughtful and kind. Before turning out the light, she went to her desk and opened the bottom drawer and looked at the blue bead, still on the loop of fishing line, that she kept there. She breathed a prayer of thanks that Jack had not heard Papa's thoughtless words about Aunt Lolly taking in strays.

As she drifted off to sleep she forced herself to think of something else. Lizzie had said she was going to enter the contest. Bernie wished she hadn't been so hasty when she had refused Alice's help with her essay. It would be hard, but now she was on her own and more determined than ever to win that contest.

7

Putting the Puzzle Together

Bernie sat at the desk in her upstairs bedroom and stared moodily out the window. The last few remaining dried leaves, which finally fell away from the trees, swirled about in circles on this windy Sunday afternoon in November. They seemed as aimless as her thoughts.

She was still smarting over the fact that Papa had dismissed her from the table for dallying over the midday meal.

"If you are not going to eat, then you can go to the kitchen and start washing the pots and pans. When everything is cleaned up, I want you to go to your room. I don't know what is the matter with you today," he had said. "You did not pay any attention during church. Your mind was elsewhere."

He was certainly correct. That morning, she had automatically taken her place in the pew, which her family occupied every Sunday. Ben went first, then Mother. Bernie came next followed by Papa with Nick on the outside aisle. Her parents had developed this arrangement from past experience. Keeping the boys apart was one sure way to keep them from creating a disturbance during the service.

Bernie was only vaguely aware of the organ playing and had to be reminded by Papa to open her hymnal to the correct page. During the rest of the service, she had restlessly plucked at a loose thread that held a button on her coat. Several times Mother had gently reached over and put her gloved hand on top of Bernie's to warn her to stop fidgeting.

Once Mother had leaned over to whisper in Bernie's ear. "Stop that before the button falls off and you lose it."

Papa had been so displeased by all of this that he covered his mouth and cleared his throat. There was no mistaking his intent. She could hear Nick snickering and that set up a chain reaction in which Papa pursed his lips in displeasure while Mother looked sternly at Ben to caution him not to join in. After church Papa hurried outside, barely pausing at the door long enough to shake the preacher's hand and tell him what a fine sermon it was. He herded them all to the car and indicated that they were to get in immediately. No one dared speak on the way home.

After the pots and pans were washed, dried, and put away following the noon meal, Bernie started to go up to her room. Papa came to the foot of the stairs and said, "Just so this day won't be a complete waste, I want you to memorize this morning's scripture lesson. You should be prepared to recite it for me before you sit down at the supper table this evening."

"Yes, sir," Bernie said, but at the top of the landing, she'd had to go back downstairs to ask Papa to remind her what book, chapter, and verses that would be.

Back upstairs, she dutifully opened her Bible to Proverbs 31:8–9. She stared at the words but could not concentrate on them anymore than she had been able to pay attention in church this morning. She soon drifted as she recalled the jumble of things that needed sorting out in her own mind. Most of this muddle revolved around what had happened at Aunt Lolly's birthday party. She recalled how annoyed she had been when she saw that Jack had been invited. She reminded herself that if he had not been invited, he could not have rescued her when she fell and became tangled in the thorny brambles on the far side of the pond. She supposed she would have had to call out for help. That would have given her brothers more reason to laugh at her and tease her unmercifully. She would never have heard the end of it.

She remembered Papa's unkind words about Aunt Lolly taking in every stray that came along. Hearing Papa's comparison of Jack to a stray animal made her think of her own criticisms of Jack's sister at the Lafayette Franchise League meeting. She understood now how awful her words must have sounded to Alice. Bernie wondered if she would ever get over that humiliation. She got up and went into the other room to splash her face with cold water. She wished she could stop thinking about it. Why did life have to be so complicated?

Finally, she remembered how upset she had been when she learned that Lizzie was going to enter the essay contest. Bernie was determined not to let Lizzie get the better of her on that score. She sat back down at her desk and took a piece of paper from the top drawer. She wrote across the top of the page: "Why the world would be a better place if women got the vote."

Bernie may have written her essay at a desk similar to the one in this photograph of a room in a house in Bloomington, Indiana, ca. 1911–15.

What could she say to convince people that she really believed those words? She certainly respected all sorts of historical giants who had led the way in trying to change some bad things happening in the world. She admired Isabel Grandison, the English woman who had come to speak at the league meeting. But Bernie had tried writing about women like this in her first essay. Alice had said that she was just copying what someone else had said. It had no feeling; it wasn't personal. So, how could Bernie make people understand that she really did care? Did she know anyone who was making the world a better place?

She turned back to the scripture she was supposed to memorize and read it again, aloud: *"Open thy mouth for the dumb in the cause of all who are appointed to destruction. Open thy mouth, judge righteously, and plead the cause of the poor and needy."*

Bernie stared at the words on the page. What did that mean? Alice had told her to ask questions, and to have a conversation with the author when she read. Bernie wondered if it was acceptable to have a conversation with the Bible? It was so hard to understand sometimes. How else was she going to know what it meant, though, if she didn't ask questions? Bernie wished that she had listened to the sermon this morning. Maybe the preacher had explained what it meant. She wished she had been listening.

She asked herself who were "the dumb"? Sheppie was a dumb animal, except for all his noisy barking. Was she supposed to speak for him? She remembered Papa's words about Aunt Lolly taking in any stray that came along. In Aunt Lolly's case, it meant far more than dogs or cats. Aunt Lolly cared about people like Jack and his sister. She had been thoughtful enough to invite Emily and her children to a family party.

It pained her to admit that even her own brothers cared about Jack. They saw his good qualities and didn't let unimportant things such as tatty clothing worry them. Why couldn't she do that? Why couldn't she care about people that way?

Her own mother cared about people. Bernie remembered something that happened one day last summer when Edna Schmidt came over to help Mother with the laundry. Edna's little granddaughter, who often came with her, clung to her grandmother's skirts.

Mother held the back door open for them. "Hello, Angelina. I'm baking cookies today." The little girl had brightened at those words and skipped happily into the kitchen.

"Come in, Edna. How are you?" her mother had said brightly.

Edna mumbled a hasty "Hello, Mrs. Epperson." But, the older woman had seemed reluctant to talk. She ducked her head and quickly picked up the wicker laundry basket that sat near the door and moved toward the washing machine.

At the time, Bernie thought it was strange that on such a hot day, Edna wore a bulky sweater and had a large scarf tied about her head. As she bent over the basket, the scarf slipped down to her shoulders. Edna quickly grabbed at it and tried to pull it back in place. Before she managed to do so, Bernie saw that Edna had a black eye and an ugly purple bruise on her cheek.

"Edna, what happened to you?" Bernie asked the woman.

"It's nothing," Edna said and turned away.

"But your eye is all puffy and you have a terrible bruise," Bernie persisted.

Angelina said, "Grandmamma told me to say that she fell down."

"How in the world could anyone get a black eye like that by falling down?"

Mother had interrupted, saying more loudly than she generally would, "Bernie, take Angelina upstairs. There are some nice dresses that you have outgrown. I laid them out on my bed. She can try them on to see if they fit. If she likes them, she can have them. I simply cannot stand to see perfectly good clothing wasted. Edna and I have a lot of work to do. We haven't got time to stand here chattering."

Now Bernie remembered the time Mr. Granger had given her a ride in his wagon—the day she had broken her arm falling out of the hayloft. He had talked about how he had seen old Mr. Schmidt knock down and beat his wife. Bernie wondered if the reason Edna wore the heavy sweater on such a hot day was to cover up other ugly bruises. She also recalled that Mr. Granger had said something about how Mr. Schmidt never worked but took the money his wife earned and spent it in the saloon.

Bernie thought about how she had seen her mother give clothing, not only to Angelina, but also to Edna. Furthermore, Mother usually cooked far too much food on the days Edna came to help. At lunchtime little Angelina sat at the kitchen table and gobbled every bite on her plate and even wiped her plate clean with a slice of bread. Mother always sent any leftovers home with Edna. Funny how Bernie had never paid much attention to this before. Now she understood Mother's actions.

As Bernie repeated the Bible verses, trying to memorize them, they began to make more and more sense. It was as though she were fitting pieces of a jigsaw puzzle together to form the picture. She realized that being "dumb" didn't always mean that a person literally could not form words, it could also mean that for some reason a person could not speak for herself.

Could that be what the scripture meant? Did these words say that we should open our mouths to speak for the poor and the needy, who dare not speak for justice? Isabel Grandison said the English women were trying to gain justice. All they wanted was to be treated fairly, to be heard. Somebody had to speak for all the people who could not make their voices heard.

This must be what Alice had been trying to get across to Bernie about caring. Bernie asked herself who she cared about. Of course she cared about her own family. But who else did she really care about?

Did she care about Edna and little Angelina? Did she care about Jack's sister? She recalled how Jack had cried out in pain when she leaned on his back the other night. She had suspected his back was tender from a whipping and she had tried to cover over any embarrassment by apologizing for her sharp elbows. She realized that Jack was a caring person, too. Even though he was treated badly by his father, he was kind to others.

Bernie picked up a pencil and began to write. The words poured out of her so fast that her fingers could hardly keep up with them:

The cartoon's caption poses the question of whether women should be allowed to vote. The answer is "No. They might disturb the existing order of things." The order of things, as portrayed by the cartoon, was corrupt politicians paying male voters to vote certain ways while women were at home, working to keep house and attend children, or out working in factories alongside children.

My father says that women should not have the vote. In fact, he says that women do not need or even want to vote. My father is a fine and honest man. He works hard and takes good care of his family. He thinks that good men should take care of women so that they won't have to get involved with politics. He believes that such things are only for men. He says that women are too pure to be part of politics. I know my father means well, but I don't think he understands.

The problem is that not all men are good men. Many of us know men who beat their wives and children. We may even know men who spend their money—money their wives earn—in saloons rather than using it to buy food for their families.

Women with husbands such as these have no one to speak for them. Women with no husbands have no one to speak for them either.

But, even women who have good husbands would like to be able to express their opinions in the voting booth. Why should men, whether they be good or bad, have the right to vote just because they are men? Why should men, good or bad, deny that basic right to women, just because they are women?

The words almost seemed to be writing themselves. It was exciting to write out her feelings this way. She continued writing until several pages were filled. The last words she put on paper were:

Who will speak for all the Ednas and Emilys and for the thousands of other unnamed women who cannot speak for themselves?

Bernie wiped away tears as she scratched out the names Edna and Emily. She substituted the fictitious names of Florence and Minnie to disguise their identities. Then she added:

Better yet, who will make the world a better place by letting any and all women speak, by being able to vote?

When Bernie went downstairs for supper that evening, not only had she memorized the scripture verses, she now understood what they meant.

PART 2

1917

8

JANUARY 1917

Serendipity

There was no way she could get out of it. Bernie had to go. There was no excuse she could come up with that would be acceptable to her mother. It did not matter what the weather was—on the second Saturday afternoon of each month Mother got dressed up, put on her best hat and gloves, and set out to visit Grandmother Epperson and Aunt Rose with Bernie in tow.

Papa may have been reading his newspaper, but that did not mean he wasn't listening to what was going on at the breakfast table. So, when Bernie, pleaded, "Why do I have to go?" Papa lowered the paper, peered at her over the edge of it, and said, "You have to go because your mother says so. Your grandmother is expecting you. She looks forward to your visits."

She saw Ben and Nick slyly glance at each other and grin.

"How come the boys don't have to go?"

"We have to work at the store," her brothers said, in gleeful unison.

She almost would have rather gone to help out at the store than be forced to go to tea with her Grandmother Epperson and Aunt Rose. Those two formidable ladies lived in a large, two-story, brick house on Ninth Street—the house where Papa had grown up.

As usual, Bernie and her mother were ushered into the front parlor by Aunt Rose. Bernie always felt as though she had entered the presence of Queen Victoria when visiting Grandmother Epperson. Grandmother sat regally in a high-back chair, her spine ramrod straight. The old woman was dressed, as usual, in a long-sleeve black dress with dozens of glossy, black buttons from her waist up to her chin. Her collar was a wisp of black lace. Her long skirt modestly covered her ankles, with only the tips of her black shoes sticking out from beneath the hem. Grandmother's white hair was pulled tightly back and knotted in a severe bun. Another bit of black lace formed a tiny cap that was perched on top of her head. It might as well have been a crown.

The room made Bernie think of something she had seen described in a book by Charles Dickens. There were heavy maroon velvet draperies hanging at the tall windows. Today, these curtains had been parted in the center but only enough to give a clue that it was daylight outside. Otherwise, the ornate room was gloomily dark. It was overly furnished with stiff settees upholstered in thick brocade. There were lavishly carved tables on which sat lamps with beaded shades. Unfortunately, the lamps gave off little light. Everywhere Bernie looked she saw frilly, hand-crocheted doilies carefully placed to prevent numerous tiny porcelain statuettes from marring the heavily polished wood surfaces. Other lacy doilies protected the upholstered backs and arms of the chairs. There were several small footstools decorated with ball fringe. Bernie was barely able to make out any pattern on the lavishly flowered wallpaper because almost every square foot was covered with gilt picture frames.

When Bernie was a little girl, Grandmother had pointed to each of the pictures and explained which Epperson—grandparent, aunt, uncle, or cousin—was portrayed. Sometimes Grandmother would quiz her, asking if she could remember the names of each of these long-dead relatives. This filled Bernie with even more dread than she felt when sticking her hand beneath a brooding hen at Grandma Mifflin's farm.

This photograph of a restored Victorian parlor gives an idea of the scene in Grandmother Epperson's parlor when Bernie and her mother went to visit.

After Mother had dutifully answered the usual questions about Papa's health, her own health, Ben's health, and Nick's health, Grandmother turned her full attention to Bernie. Bernie was about to take a bite of what looked like a delicious cream tart, but quickly put it down on the delicate china plate she was holding.

"How is your broken arm, Bernice?" Grandmother Epperson asked, apparently forgetting that she had asked that same question during every visit for the last six months.

"The cast has been off quite a while," Bernie said. "It was off in time for my birthday last August."

"Has the arm healed properly?"

"Yes, Grandmother, it healed nicely." The truth of the matter was that it was not fine. The break had been severe, and the doctor had said her elbow might never be able to fully unbend. He had also told her that when cold weather set in, the joint might ache. He had been right, but she wasn't about to tell that to Grandmother Epperson. Bernie stared at her mother, trying to send a message that she didn't want to discuss it. Mother was looking down at her teacup and seemed not to notice. Bernie suspected that Mother didn't want to get involved in this matter anymore than she did.

"Well, it was a very foolish thing that you did, Bernice. You were fortunate to have received only a broken arm as a result of that little escapade."

Bernie tightened her lips. It was all she could do to keep from reminding her grandmother that she was not the only one involved in that "little escapade." Her brothers had been the ones who thought up the flying-from-the-barn-experiment. Bernie sighed deeply while Grandmother stirred her tea with a dainty silver spoon. She hoped that was the end of the discussion.

However, Grandmother continued, "Speaking of escapades, you have started off this new year in an interesting manner. I read your essay that was published in the *Daily Courier* a few days ago. I am sure by now the entire town has read it."

The minute she heard the word escapade, Bernie knew she was not going to receive any congratulations from Grandmother about winning the essay contest. Grandmother was not pleased by Bernie's first excursion into the world of journalism. It was the same deflating response that Bernie had received from Papa.

Bernie had been so full of great dreams when she had submitted her essay to the Lafayette Franchise League judges in November. She could hardly wait through the long month of December for the announcement. She had been certain that if she won, her family would be proud of her. However, she had been completely crushed when Papa looked up from his newspaper that morning after reading her article. He had rustled the paper and cleared his throat vociferously. He had not smiled at all. She had waited until he spoke. It was not at all the reception she had fantasized. Instead of pride in her accomplishment, he was angry. He stood up and walked into the kitchen. He wadded the newspaper into a tight ball and tossed it into the wastepaper box beside the kitchen stove.

She was so disappointed that she could hardly force herself to go to school that morning. She had to put it out of her mind to keep from breaking down in tears during class. When she got home from school that afternoon, she made certain that no one was around before she tiptoed into the kitchen to retrieve the newspaper. She thought perhaps she might take some small comfort from the *Daily Courier*'s editor, who wrote the glowing praise, "Such talent in one so young," as well as predicting "a bright future for the writer."

She was glad to find that the wadded up paper was still in the box, but when she smoothed out the page where her essay was printed, she discovered that the article was missing. Her essay had been carefully clipped out.

Now, here she sat in Grandmother Epperson's front parlor and received yet another scolding. Grandmother Epperson could have been parroting Papa's very words when she said, "I don't know what in the world you were thinking to prompt you to write something

While many women fought for the right to vote, a large number of women opposed women's suffrage. Like many anti-suffragists, these women believed their place was in the home.

like this. You have exposed our entire family to ridicule. Do you have any idea how hard your Grandfather Epperson worked to establish his business in this town? He had to struggle to establish his good name, especially during the difficult economic times of the 1890s. Some other businessmen in town were forced to close their doors. They could not find the money to keep operating. Indeed, your grandfather almost went bankrupt, but he managed to pay back everything he owed to all of his creditors. Our name stands for something honorable in this town. Now your clever little article has. . . ." Grandmother was so overwrought, she struggled for words. "You have embarrassed your father—your parents, as well as those poor women you wrote about."

This was a new accusation. Papa had not said anything about that. What did Grandmother mean by saying that she had embarrassed those poor women?

"But I changed their names. How could they have been embarrassed?" Bernie said defensively.

Grandmother peered at Bernie over the top of the little gold-framed glasses perched on her narrow nose. "Don't you think that everyone in this town knows exactly who you were describing? It does not matter whether you called them Florence and Minnie or Edna and Emily. People know who they are, and people talk."

Grandmother paused momentarily, but Bernie had the feeling she was only getting started.

Aunt Rose stood up abruptly and said, "Bernice, I need some help clearing these tea things away. Would you please carry that tray into the kitchen for me?"

Bernie jumped up so quickly in her eagerness to escape this ordeal, she almost knocked over a crystal vase. She grabbed the tray and hurried out into the hallway leading to the kitchen. Her heart was pounding with relief that she had not broken one of her grandmother's treasures.

Once they reached the kitchen, Aunt Rose said, "Bernie, it's time you learned a few things."

At first, Bernie thought she had escaped from one scolding in the parlor only to face another reprimand from Aunt Rose in the kitchen.

"Come with me," Aunt Rose ordered, and led the way up a flight of narrow backstairs to the second floor.

Bernie obediently followed her aunt into a small room at the top of the stairway. She saw Aunt Rose standing in front of a chest of drawers with her back toward Bernie. She did not turn immediately. Bernie waited, bracing herself for what was to come.

She waited for what seemed an eternity, looking around. Bernie had never been in her aunt's room before. She thought, in wonder, at how different it was from all the other rooms in the house. It was so plain, like a stern reproach to the rest of the house.

There was a small iron bedstead in the corner covered with a simple white bedspread. Plain white cotton curtains hung at the window. There was a bedside table with a small lamp and a bookcase crammed with books. Only one picture hung on the wall, placed over the chest of drawers. Aunt Rose stood staring at it.

At last, Aunt Rose finally turned to face her. To Bernie's surprise she saw that her aunt had been crying. Aunt Rose approached her. She reached out and took Bernie by the shoulders, and looking straight into her eyes, said, "Bernie, I just want you to know how proud I was of you when I read your essay in the newspaper. I must have read it a dozen times over."

Aunt Rose wrapped her arms around her niece and hugged her. Bernie had no idea what to say or do. Aunt Rose had always seemed to be a withdrawn, distant person. She appeared to be very prim and proper, like Grandmother Epperson. Bernie felt as though she was meeting a person she had never known.

"Forgive me," Aunt Rose said, and then stood back. "I didn't mean to come at you that way. It is just that I couldn't bear to hear my mother scolding you for what you wrote. Your words needed to be written. In your essay you asked who spoke for the Florences and Minnies of this world. That question needed to be asked. There are so many poor women who need someone who dares to speak out for them."

After another tearful pause, Aunt Rose continued, "There are also some other women who are not poor, in terms of this world's wealth, but who need someone to speak for them, too. These are the women who don't have the courage to speak up for themselves."

Aunt Rose turned back to the chest and knelt on the braided rug in front of it. She opened the bottom drawer, withdrew something, and handed it to Bernie. It was a photograph of a young man—a very handsome young man. Bernie had no idea where this conversation was leading, so she waited until Aunt Rose spoke. When she did, it was as though a dam had burst and a waterfall of words spilled from her lips.

"I was seventeen when I met him," Aunt Rose said. "He was a talented artist, but his talents were unrecognized at that time. He traveled about from town to town. An itinerant artist they called him. He painted miniature portraits. When he came to our town I asked him to paint one of me. I planned to give it to my parents as a gift."

Aunt Rose pulled something else from the bottom drawer and handed it to Rose. It was a delicate little painting in a gold frame.

"Is this you?" Bernie asked in wonder.

"Hard to believe, isn't it?" Aunt Rose stated. "It is probably hard for you to see much left of me in the woman I have become."

Bernie continued to stare at the tiny painting. Her aunt was right. She had no idea her aunt had once been so beautiful. Bernie wondered what had happened to that young man Aunt Rose had obviously cared so much about.

American artist John Henry Brown painted this miniature portrait, titled The Lady, *ca. 1890 with watercolor on ivory. This type of portrait was truly tiny. With its frame, this one measures a mere 3½ inches high and 2¾ inches wide. Many miniature portraits were worn as jewelry in lockets, bracelets, and broaches. Aunt Rose's miniature portrait may have looked similar to this one.*

It was as though Aunt Rose had heard her unspoken question.

"His name was Ralph. He asked me to marry him. My parents were absolutely horrified. They overwhelmed me with all the reasons I could not possibly marry him. They said that I was too young. They said that he had no money to support a wife. Even worse, he wanted to go out West and paint the scenic wonders. Oh, they agreed that he did have talent, but he would not be able to provide a proper life for their daughter. I was not strong enough to stand up to them. I had no one to speak for me, except for Ralph, and of course they would not listen to him."

After wiping away a few more tears, Aunt Rose continued, "He pleaded with me to run away with him, but I was the dutiful stay-at-home daughter. I was not like your father. He had the courage to speak up when he wanted to marry your mother, no matter how unsuitable they thought she might be. It was only when your father promised to stay right here and take over the family business that they relented."

"But, what happened to Ralph?" Bernie asked, so anxious to hear more about Aunt Rose's story that she barely heard the words about her own father. "Did he go west?"

"Yes, he did," Aunt Rose said, her words so soft Bernie could barely hear them.

"Did you ever hear from him again?"

"He said he would send for me as soon as he made his fortune, but he never wrote. At least, that was what I thought because I never received a letter from him. I was heartbroken."

"Do you suppose he ever made a fortune?" Bernie wondered.

Aunt Rose nodded. "Perhaps not a great fortune, but he did make quite a name for himself with his paintings of the West. One time your grandmother and I went to Chicago on the train to do some shopping. There I saw a poster in a window. It advertised an art exhibition of his works. When my mother went back to the hotel to rest, I managed to slip away and go to the gallery where his paintings were displayed. As chance would have it, he was there. We had lunch together and talked. I learned that he had written many letters, which I never received. He did not know why I never responded and thought I had changed my mind about him. I realized then that my parents must have intercepted his letters to me. But of course, it was too late. By this time he was married and had two children."

Aunt Rose had a faraway look in her eyes. Bernie could only imagine what she was thinking. "He gave me one of his paintings."

Bernie glanced at the only thing adorning the wall of Aunt Rose's room. "Is this the one?"

Aunt Rose nodded. Bernie walked over and looked more closely at it. It was a beautiful painting, depicting a brilliant sun setting behind the tall jagged peaks of western mountains. This was a picture of the life Aunt Rose could have shared with the man she loved—if she had only had the courage to speak for herself and go with him.

When she turned back to her aunt, Bernie felt tears in her eyes. Aunt Rose was weeping. As Bernie looked at her, she realized that Aunt Rose's eyes were the exact same hazel color as her own.

The two of them stood quietly until Aunt Rose said, "The Aunt Roses of the world need someone to speak for them, too. You can do that. Whenever anyone tries to discourage you, just think of me."

Bernie nodded. She wanted to tell Aunt Rose how wretched she felt, but for once she had no words.

Aunt Rose took Bernie's hand, squeezed it and said, "Enough of this. We'd better get back downstairs. They will wonder what we have been doing all this time."

Bernie hoped Mother was not having to endure any more of Grandmother's angry tirade. "What do you suppose they are talking about now?"

"Your grandmother is probably showing off my latest handiwork," Aunt Rose laughed. "Another crocheted doily."

Bernie was giggling when she said, "I hope she's not suggesting to Mother that you teach me how to crochet." Bernie paused, hoping that she hadn't offended her aunt. She quickly added, "Not that the doilies you make aren't nice. They really are very pretty."

Aunt Rose's shoulders begin to shake and Bernie realized that her aunt was trying to hold back laughter. The two of them collapsed against each other giggling uncontrollably. Bernie thought how much Aunt Rose sounded like her own girlfriends at school. It was a few moments before they were able to regain their composure.

"I have a confession to make," Bernie said softly. "I did not want to come over to visit Grandmother today."

"That is certainly understandable," Aunt Rose said.

"But I am so glad I did," Bernie added quickly. "I thought today was going to be dreadful. And it was at first, but I found something unexpected—something better."

"There is a word for that," Aunt Rose told her. "It is called serendipity."

Bernie repeated the word. "Serendipity." She said it one more time to fix it in her mind. Its five syllables rolled across her tongue like the mellow taste of butterscotch. What a delicious word it was.

When Bernie and Aunt Rose finally returned to the parlor, Bernie saw her mother and grandmother look quizzically at them. Bernie dared not look at Aunt Rose. She was afraid they would burst out laughing again. Then Grandmother would really have a reason to scold her.

As Bernie and her mother returned home, Bernie went over the events of the afternoon in her mind. She thought about the many things Aunt Rose had told her. One of those things stood out in her memory: "Your father had the courage to speak up when he wanted to marry your mother even though our parents thought she was unsuitable for him."

Bernie had been so engrossed in the story of Aunt Rose's sad romance that she hadn't thought much about that statement at the time. Now she wondered, what could it have meant? Someday she would have to ask Aunt Rose more about that. Or, perhaps Aunt Lolly would know.

She was mulling this over when Mother looked at her questioningly. "Did you say something, Bernie?"

Bernie hoped she had not spoken aloud without realizing it. Quickly she replied, "Oh, I learned a new word today and I don't want to forget it. Aunt Rose taught it to me."

Then another thought popped into her head. Serendipity was possibly a word that even her smart cousin, Lizzie, had never heard of. Bernie smiled happily.

9

Trouble Brewing

It had seemed like a good idea when Bernie first thought of inviting Aunt Rose to attend the Lafayette Franchise League meeting with her. It had taken a lot of convincing. Aunt Rose had all sorts of reasons why she would not be able to attend.

"There is no way I could convince your Grandmother Epperson to stay alone in the evening," she said. "Not even for a couple of hours."

"Bring her to the meeting with you," Bernie suggested.

Aunt Rose rolled her eyes. "I can't even imagine it. Can you?"

Bernie shook her head no. She could not imagine it. "Why not ask Edna Schmidt to come and stay with her while you are away?"

"But what can I tell her I am going to do that evening? If she had any idea what I was planning to do, she would have our handyman nail every door in the house shut. I would never be able to go anywhere again."

"Tell her you are going to attend an educational program," Bernie suggested. "That is certainly truthful."

As it turned out, the league meeting was much more than educational. Bernie was surprised to learn that there were several strong disagreements within the ranks of the members about which direction their group should take. Voices here and there throughout the meeting hall called out their ideas.

One person raised the issue of keeping the peace. "I believe the United States is going to enter the war in Europe. It is up to us to do everything we can to prevent it."

"Don't forget about the temperance movement," said a woman. She wore a white rosette with a trailing ribbon pinned to her jacket. Bernie knew this identified her as a member of a group called the Woman's Christian

Temperance Union that worked to ban the sale of liquor. There was a smattering of applause. The woman turned and nodded her head in appreciation for their support as she sat down.

"What about child labor and orphanages?" Another woman called out. "Don't we care about the children?"

"Let's work harder to close the sweatshops where women work long hours under terrible conditions. Some of them have even died."

After applause had died down following the latter suggestion, yet another voice added, "We care about all of these things, but we simply cannot spread ourselves too thin. We must stay focused if we are going to reach our goal. This is the Lafayette Franchise League, part of the National American Woman Suffrage Association. Our purpose is and always has been to get the right to vote for women. Those other things, worthy as they are, can come later." This time the applause was louder and lasted longer.

The members were becoming more agitated. "Can't you see that these things are all parts of the whole? If women get the vote, they must be prepared to use it to stamp out the evils in our society."

There was a swelling undertone of supporting and opposing voices.

The leader pounded her gavel on the podium. "Order! Order! We'll not get any of these important things done if we don't act in an orderly fashion. Now, one at a time. Raise your hands, please, if you desire to speak."

Bernie had never witnessed the group behaving in this manner before. She hoped that this wasn't making a bad impression on Aunt Rose. She might not want to return.

Someone raised the issue of how they could get more attention for any of their causes. "Remember how Isabel Grandison told us that the English women couldn't get the newspapers to notice them or take them seriously?"

"Well, we certainly had plenty of publicity when the *Daily Courier* printed the winning essay for our contest. Everyone in town was talking about it."

That was exactly what Papa and Grandmother Epperson had said. Bernie slumped low in her seat remembering what a painful experience that was. She didn't even dare glance in Aunt Rose's direction.

The speaker went on to say that what the group needed was more such publicity. "We need to do something that will make everyone sit up and take notice of our cause."

Someone in the back of the room said, "I have a suggestion. We could march around the courthouse square, carrying banners."

Buttons with the rallying cry "Votes for Women," such as this one, attracted attention to the suffrage movement. Wearing one was a way for women to show that they supported women's right to vote.
GIFT OF SARA SKILLEN COOK ESTATE, INDIANA HISTORICAL SOCIETY COLLECTIONS

"Why stop with a march around the courthouse? We ought to go to Washington, DC. Other franchise leagues are planning to march for President Wilson's inauguration in March. If we send a delegation, maybe we could get our picture in the newspapers."

Several voices agreed that this was a good idea. "How large should such a delegation be?"

"Why not invite everyone who belongs to the league?"

"Yes. Yes. We could all travel together on the train. That certainly would make an impression on this town."

"How many people do you think we could we get to go?"

"Why limit the trip to our members? If each one of us asked one other person, we could double the crowd. I say, the more the better."

"Everyone here tonight who would go on such a trip, raise your hand."

Alice, Lizzie, and Aunt Lolly immediately stood up, held their hands high, and looked around. Bernie watched as more and more women stood with raised hands. The chair took a count. There were twenty-seven women who said they would go.

Someone went to the piano and began to pound out, "The Battle Hymn of the Republic." Those who were standing began to sing the words to that stirring anthem.

"Come on," urged the chair. "We've got to have more people than that. We ought to fill an entire railroad carriage."

"Why stop with one carriage? Make it two."

"We'll take anybody who wants to go. Encourage a friend—two friends—five friends to make the trip with us. Just think about it—this is a great opportunity to visit our nation's capital."

"Let's set a goal of one hundred people to make the journey with us."

A voice near the rear suggested, "We could gather at the courthouse and march from there to the railroad station on the day we leave. That should get some publicity."

"If we want publicity we will need someone to write articles for publication in the *Daily Courier*."

"What better person to do this job than the bright young lady who won our essay contest? She certainly has a way with words." Bernie was surprised to hear a ripple of applause that turned into a wave of approval.

Someone shouted, "Stand up, Miss Epperson. Take a bow."

"Stand up," Lizzie insisted, without a trace of envy even though she had not won the contest. Bernie knew that was one of the things that made everyone love Lizzie so much. There wasn't a jealous bone in her body.

Reluctantly, Bernie got to her feet as the applause rolled over her. Then she sat down again quickly, her face flaming with embarrassment at the attention.

The woman at the piano called out, "We can sing as we march. Just think of it. One hundred voices strong for women and the vote."

Bernie heard the piano begin to play again. This time it was the melody for "The March of the Women." Those who knew the words started to sing:

Shout, shout, up with your song!
Cry with the wind, for the dawn is breaking;

Women in Hebron, Porter County, Indiana, took to the streets in 1919 to spread their belief that they should be allowed to vote.

March, march, swing you along,
Wide blows our banner, and hope is waking.

Bernie hadn't been a member of the league long enough to have learned all the words, but she chimed in whenever she could remember a line or two. More voices joined in the song:

Song with its story, dreams with their glory
Lo! they call, and glad is their word!
Loud and louder it swells,
Thunder of freedom, the voice of the Lord!

Bernie looked around and realized that she was one of the few persons who was still seated. She would have to go if she were to be the publicity person. If Aunt Lolly was going maybe she could get permission to go also. She took a deep breath and stood, hand raised as she sang loudly:

Long, long—we in the past
Cowered in dread from the light of heaven,
Strong, strong—stand we at last,
Fearless in faith and with sight new given.
Strength with its beauty, Life with its duty,
(Hear the voice, oh hear and obey!)
These, these—beckon us on!
Open your eyes to the blaze of day.

By the third verse, Bernie could remember no more of the words, so she just hummed the stirring tune as she listened to the others sing:

Comrades—ye who have dared
First in the battle to strive and sorrow!
Scorned, spurned—nought have ye cared,
Raising your eyes to a wider morrow,
Ways that are weary, days that are dreary,
Toil and pain by faith ye have borne;
Hail, hail—victors ye stand,
Wearing the wreath that the brave have worn!

The music filled the hall, seeming to rattle the windows and shake the very timbers of the roof above them. It didn't matter that the piano was old and slightly out of tune. It didn't matter that not everyone knew the words. Bernie thought she had never heard more beautiful or exciting music in her entire life. She felt as though she had become part of the song herself. She felt Aunt Rose grasp her left hand. Her aunt's other hand was raised high in the air. Aunt Rose had picked up the tune and was singing at the top of her voice. Although she wasn't singing the words, she was chanting "La—la—la—la."

Bernie asked, "Aunt Rose, what are you doing?"

Aunt Rose was grinning widely—an expression Bernie had never expected to see on her aunt's face—and her eyes twinkled with excitement. "I'm getting ready to go to Washington, DC."

"But what will Grandmother say when you ask her if you can go?"

"I don't think I shall ask. I will simply tell her what I am going to do. I have a lot of lost time to make up for."

Others who knew it, sang the last verse.

Women's suffrage meetings attracted women from varying backgrounds. They allowed women to voice their opinions, debate issues, and organize events. This photograph shows a meeting of women in Washington, DC, ca. 1910, rallying for a proposed amendment that they called the Susan B. Anthony Amendment for the enfranchisement of women.

Life, strife—those two are one,
Naught can ye win but by faith and daring.
On, on—that ye have done
But for the work of today preparing.
Firm in reliance, laugh at defiance,
(Laugh in hope, for sure is the end)
March, march—many as one,
Shoulder to shoulder and friend to friend.

When the meeting was over, Bernie's head was spinning. Things had progressed much faster and much farther than she had expected. She had allowed herself to be swept up in the excitement of the moment. Papa was not going to be happy about this. Was she about to get herself in hot water again? Well, if Aunt Rose was prepared to take a giant step, Bernie knew she would too. Of course, unlike Aunt Rose, Bernie would not be able to just announce that she was going. The big hurdle would be to get Papa to permit her to go and help to pay her way. Or, perhaps it would be wiser to approach Mother first and try to convince her. It would help that both Aunt Lolly and Aunt Rose would be making the trip.

10

"A Journey of a Thousand Miles Begins with a Single Step"

Bernie could hardly believe that she and the other women were already on their way home from Washington, DC. They had planned their march for what had seemed like forever. But once the big moment arrived, time seemed to have moved at lightning speed. The days of the trip to the nation's capital had flashed by quickly, especially the fourth day.

The run-in with the police had happened so fast and was so unexpected that many of those moments were blurred in Bernie's mind. She was glad to be back on the train because she needed time to sort out the events in her mind. Bernie turned to a blank page in her tablet and began to make notes. The swaying motion of the train made it difficult to write. However, she knew that she must get her thoughts down on paper as soon as possible. A lot had happened and much of it was confusing. She was afraid she would leave something out.

When the trip began, almost a week ago, she had planned to keep a daily journal. By the second night in DC, she was so tired that she went to sleep the minute her head touched the pillow in the hotel room. Before long she gave up and decided she would have to be content with making random notes of her impressions. She told herself she could fill in the details later. Now it was almost like turning the pages of a photo album as she reviewed each day in her mind. Strangely, at the same time, it seemed as though she had dreamed the entire adventure.

On the first day, some members of the group insisted that they go to see the cherry trees around the Tidal Basin. Five years before, the Japanese government had gifted the three thousand trees to the United States. Bernie was disappointed at what she felt was a frivolous attitude. After all, they had traveled such a long distance to be part of a march to help women get the vote.

The league's president had wisely stated that it would be best to get the sightseeing done immediately. That way their focus could be on the more serious purpose that had brought them to the nation's capital.

Bernie understood that seeing the nation's capital had been one of the things about the trip that made it possible to recruit so many women to go along as part of their delegation. It certainly had been one of the things that had helped her convince her mother, who in turn had convinced Papa to let her make this journey. Bernie felt a bit guilty that she had emphasized the sightseeing to him and had hardly mentioned the women's march.

On the actual day of the march Bernie was barely able to contain her nervousness as their delegation took its place with groups of women from other states. The women were marching at the second inauguration of President Woodrow Wilson. It was a cold, rainy day, and the marchers wore raincoats and hats. They lined up in rows, each member wearing a wide, purple, white, and gold sash tied diagonally across her chest, indicating that they were part of the national women's suffrage movement. The Lafayette Franchise League

In 1917 suffragists from across the country united to picket, march, and protest at the White House and around Washington, DC. This photo is from the "Grand Picket" march, which took place during the day leading up to President Woodrow Wilson's second inauguration on March 4, 1917.

marched behind women carrying signs that said Indiana in big letters. All the marchers were grouped according to their home states, but the women from Indiana were especially proud. They wanted everyone to know where they were from because their state had just given women the partial right to vote in Indiana in February.

Most of the marchers carried a sign. Some women helped to carry large banners that almost reached from curb to curb, proclaiming slogans such as "Shoulder to Shoulder, Friend to Friend" and "Fearless Women Make a Fearless Society." One of the banners posed the question: "How Long Must Women Wait for Their God-Given Rights?"

Each of the women carried a small American flag. Some of them waved a toothbrush high in the air. Bernie explained to Aunt Rose that this was in honor of Dame Ethel Smyth, the English composer who had written the song, "The March of the Women." When Smyth was jailed for breaking an anti-suffrage politician's window, she had stood at her prison window and used her toothbrush as a baton, directing the women standing in the prison yard below singing her stirring anthem.

Bernie was proud that her group had learned all the words to every verse of the song so they could sing it as they marched along Pennsylvania Avenue in DC. To hear and be a part of so many voices all raised in the same tune made her feel as though she were floating in a cloud of heavenly music.

The march ended in front of the White House. Bernie noticed several women chaining themselves to the fence. As she stood taking it all in, she felt something mushy hit her forehead and run down her face. She put her hand up to find out what it was. It was a gooey blob of a half-eaten peach. As Lizzie tried to wipe it off for her, another missile came flying through the air. This was a dirt clod. It hit Bernie on the shoulder. Another hit Lizzie in the back.

Aunt Lolly said, "Don't worry about it, girls. These are badges of honor. Wear them proudly."

Suddenly Bernie saw four burly men dash from the curb. They headed toward an older woman who was with a group of marchers from another state. The men tried to snatch the sign from her hands, but she held on tightly and struggled with them. They finally got the better of her and knocked her roughly to the ground.

Two other women marchers burst from the Indiana ranks and went to help the woman who had been attacked. Bernie gasped when she realized that the two women who hurried to assist were Aunt Lolly and Aunt Rose.

Some women who fought for suffrage were arrested and sent to prison for voicing their opinions. In this 1917 photograph, suffragist Mary Winsor from Pennsylvania holds a sign declaring that women who had been arrested should not be treated as criminals. Winsor was jailed for sixty days after picketing in 1917.

"Are you all right?" Aunt Lolly asked the woman, who nodded as she patted her white hair back in place.

"Shame on you!" Aunt Rose shouted at the men, who turned to run away when the police showed up.

One of the policemen said to the three women, "You will have to move along or I'll take the lot of you to jail."

Aunt Lolly put her hands on her hips and faced the law officers. "And just what were we doing that would make you arrest us?"

Aunt Rose added, "Why aren't you chasing after those cowards who knocked this defenseless woman to the ground?"

A cheer went up from several marchers who had gathered round to watch the scene.

It was then that a young man with an identification card in his hat band rushed up to snap their picture. His card read *Washington Post*. The newspaper reporter asked their names and jotted them down in a small notebook.

The next day Bernie's aunts were startled to see a large photograph of themselves spread across the first page of the paper. The headline proclaimed, "Fearless Suffragettes Face Down Hoodlums and Police." The photograph clearly showed Aunt Lolly standing almost nose to nose with the policeman and Aunt Rose turned and shouting at the bullies. The caption beneath the picture recounted the story of the confrontation. It also printed their names and told where they were from.

Alice commented, "Well, our league wanted publicity, and we certainly got it."

Bernie mumbled under her breath, "Thank goodness this picture is in a Washington, DC, newspaper and not in the *Daily Courier*." She could imagine what Papa would say if he could see this. She scanned the picture carefully to be certain that she had not been in it and offered up another prayer of relief. Then she remembered that she had accepted the responsibility of reporting on this at home.

As she sat on the train and remembered the excitement, she thought how it was going to be tricky to submit an account of what had happened. She was not able to work a way out of her dilemma before the excitement of the past few days took its toll. She fell asleep to the rhythmic clatter of the train wheels on the track.

When she awakened, she realized that her head was resting heavily against Aunt Rose's shoulder. She looked across the aisle and saw Lizzie stretched out across the laps of Alice and their mother. Aunt Lolly's head had slumped on her chest. They were all sound asleep as were most of the other travelers in their group.

"I'm sorry," Bernie whispered to Aunt Rose as she sat up. "I didn't mean to bother you."

"You were no bother. I rather liked having you sleep on my shoulder," Aunt Rose said. "It reminded me of how much I used to enjoy holding you when you were a tiny baby. I used to beg to take you out in your buggy for walks all over town to show you off to people. I was so proud of my beautiful niece."

"I wish I could remember." Bernie felt wistful that she had not been aware of the experience. She hesitated for a moment before asking timidly, "Did Grandmother and Grandfather Epperson like me?"

Aunt Rose turned to stare at her. "Of course they did. Whatever in the world made you ask a question like that?"

"Grandmother is always so cross with me. She doesn't ever seem to be pleased with anything I do."

"They thought you were perfect," Aunt Rose assured her.

"Were they happy with me even though my mother was a Mifflin?"

"I don't think that thought ever crossed their minds."

Bernie continued to press the issue. "How could that be? Don't you remember that you told me how they did not want Papa to marry my mother?"

Aunt Rose sighed audibly. "Quite frankly, your Grandfather and Grandmother Epperson did not think that someone from the Mifflin family was a suitable match for their son."

"Why was that?"

Aunt Rose couldn't suppress a smile. "You will have to admit that your Great Uncle Charley Mifflin is quite a character."

"But he was a war hero who rode with General Lew Wallace."

"He does spin quite an entertaining yarn, doesn't he? To hear him tell it, one would think he won the Civil War single-handedly."

"I think they should be proud of him. I know he is Nick's hero. Nick hopes the United States will join the war in Europe. A lot of people say we will. Nick wants a chance to be a great soldier like Uncle Charley. It is exciting to think that he fought alongside General Wallace."

"I suspect the closest your Great-Uncle Charley ever got to General Wallace was one day, a long time ago, when he and a bunch of loafers were hired to go down to Crawfordsville and pull the weeds from the Wallaces' flower beds."

Bernie was stunned. She sat thinking this over. "How do you know this?"

"You must remember," Aunt Rose said, "Lafayette isn't such a big town that people don't know each other's business—and they love to talk about it."

"But why should Uncle Charley's war stories make the Mifflins unsuitable for marriage with the Eppersons?"

Aunt Rose appeared hesitant and extremely uncomfortable. "It's not just that."

"What else? Why didn't Grandmother and Grandfather Epperson want Papa to marry Mother?"

"I shouldn't have said anything," Aunt Rose replied.

"You have to tell me. I want to know," Bernie insisted. "Was it because the Mifflins have red hair?"

At that, Aunt Rose laughed so loudly she had to cover her mouth. "Good grief, Bernie. It's your Aunt Lolly's side of the family that has the beautiful red hair. Your mother and Uncle Leroy have hair the same color as yours. In fact, your mother was a real dark-haired beauty. Your father was head over heels in love with her."

Bernie struggled to even imagine her parents as two young people in love. Aunt Rose continued, "Your mother had quite a flair for the dramatic. Whenever there was a program, she was always the one called upon to recite poetry or give a dramatic reading. She had a lovely singing voice, too. She sang in the church choir."

"Then why wouldn't Grandfather and Grandmother Epperson want Papa to marry her?"

Aunt Rose had a faraway look in her eyes. "Well, you know how they are—how my father was and how my mother still is."

Bernie thought that over, but still was not satisfied. She felt certain that Aunt Rose was not telling her the entire story. She waited.

"Just let me say that your father was very brave. He stood up to our parents and told them that he was determined to marry the woman he loved. I only wish I could have had that much courage. If I had, my life would be very much different than it is today."

With that, Aunt Rose leaned back and closed her eyes. Bernie knew that was the end of the matter—at least for now.

Bernie could not help but think what a strange journey this had been. She turned back to the notes she was making for the article she would submit to the local paper. She started with their arrival in the nation's capital. She described sights such as the Washington Monument, the thousands of cherry trees, and the magnificent buildings, including the capitol building. Then she attempted to describe the march and the gathering outside the White House. She wondered if it would be honest reporting if she ignored the women's encounter with the police.

Before long, she digressed as she considered the many interesting people she had met along the way. Each one was so different. They were young and old. Some women brought their young daughters to march side-by-side with them. There were women from many places and walks of life. She realized that each of them came from many different kinds of homes. None of their stories would be the same. Even friends and neighbors on this train, people who belonged to the same league she belonged to at home, were unique. Each had come along because of her own personal experience. For whatever reason, they had dared to stand up for women's right to vote. They had reached this understanding by traveling along different paths just as she had. Yet, they stood shoulder to shoulder, united in a common cause.

Bernie hoped she would be able to express all of this in a way that others would be able to feel what she felt. She wanted to speak for the Ednas and Emilys who couldn't be there.

11

Peace and Quiet?

Back home again, Bernie realized she had been mistaken when she first saw the photograph that was published in the *Washington Post*. She had been grateful that the photograph of Aunt Lolly and Aunt Rose would not be seen by readers of the *Daily Courier*. Somehow, she had failed to realize that local newspapers often reprinted pictures from other papers far away.

When she came down to breakfast on her first morning back at home, she saw Papa's copy of the *Daily Courier* lying beside his coffee cup. There, on the front page, was the photograph. She almost turned around and fled back upstairs, but she knew that she would have to face the consequences sooner or later. It might as well be now. Perhaps it wouldn't be too bad or last too long because Papa would have to leave soon to go to work. It was a point of pride with Papa that he was never late opening his store.

"Good morning, Papa." She tried to make her voice as cheerful as possible while she waited for the eruption. She took her place in the chair beside Nick and across from Ben, who sat next to Mother. She was greeted with silence. Silence from Papa. Deafening silence from the boys. Neither one of them so much as glanced in her direction.

She continued to wait until Mother asked, "Would you like milk for your cereal?"

"I'm not very hungry," Bernie said.

"You need to keep up your strength," Mother insisted.

Bernie thought she detected a snicker from Nick, but it was stifled immediately as he asked for another biscuit and the blackberry jam.

Bernie took this as an ominous sign. Perhaps she would need her strength for when Papa got ready to do or say whatever he had in mind. She began to think of what she could offer in her own defense.

She might say, "Papa, I did nothing to be ashamed of. We were only there to speak up for our rights—rights that every woman deserves. We weren't arrested. We did not have to go to jail. I did not get my picture in the paper. I did nothing wrong."

In her heart of hearts, however, Bernie had to admit that she had done something wrong. She had not told the entire story when she had pleaded her case to be allowed to make the trip to Washington, DC. She had deliberately let Mother and Papa think it was only a sightseeing trip. Technically, not telling the whole truth was the same as telling a lie. She remembered that their minister had once preached about sins of omission.

She could confess that she knew she had been wrong and now she repented. She could throw herself on his mercy. What would he do? She could really only remember one occasion when he had actually spanked her. She was four years old and had hidden in the closet under the front stair. She had not answered when he called her. She had fallen asleep there. Later, when she awakened and emerged, she saw her parents standing in the front hallway. Papa's face was ghostly white and pinched looking. Her mother was crying.

Mother had run to her and wrapped her arms about her. "Oh Bernie! We looked everywhere and couldn't find you. Where have you been all this time? We thought you were lost. We were so frightened."

The expression on Papa's face was one that a little girl could not understand. He stepped forward and picked her up. He carried her into the parlor and put her across his knee. He gave her one swat with his open hand. It had not been much of a swat. Bernie had barely felt it because of her skirt and petticoat, but she had bawled loudly as though she were being murdered. Mother had come running to see what was happening. She screamed and pleaded with Papa to stop. Bernie had looked up at Papa and saw that tears were running down his face. Then he pulled her close to him and hugged her. She remembered thinking that parents were strange people, indeed.

Now, she sat at the breakfast table and wondered what would happen next. When she dared to look at her father she thought, with surprise, how weary he seemed. She pushed back her chair and stood up. She went to kneel beside his chair, putting her head on his arm. She felt his hand touch the top of her head. He patted it gently. She stayed where she was until the boys pushed back

HIS DAUGHTER!
And he thought she was "just a little girl"

This political cartoon depicts how Bernie's father must have felt when he saw his sister's picture in the newspaper and realized his daughter was a strong and independent young woman who held opinions regarding women's suffrage that she was willing to fight for.

their chairs and left the room. Mother came around the table and kissed her. After that, she left the room, too.

Bernie looked up at her father and said, "I'm glad to be home, Papa."

Papa picked up the newspaper, shook it, cleared his throat and said in a bewildered tone. "My own sister. I could have expected such a thing from your Aunt Lolly, but I never would have dreamed that your Aunt Rose would do something like this."

Papa scooted his chair back and pulled Bernie up onto his lap. She looked at him and smiled. "I'm much too big to be sitting on your lap."

"Don't say that. You will always be my little girl. At least, I guess that is what I have been saying to myself. But, I need to face the fact that you are no longer a child. You are a young lady with a mind of your own. A very determined mind, it seems."

She leaned her head back against his shoulder. "I love you, Papa."

"I love you, too," he said and kissed her on the forehead. "I want you to know that it is not always easy for me to know what to do, but I am proud of you. You are very much like your mother."

Bernie turned to look at him. She thought she saw a sprinkling of gray hairs at his temples that she had not noticed before. She wondered how many of those she was responsible for.

"I'll try not to be such a problem in the future," she said.

She felt a chuckle rumble down deep inside of Papa's chest. He didn't have to speak for her to know that he expected her to keep him wondering what in the world she would do next.

"I would like to try to make this a better year for you," she promised. Then she had an idea. "Your birthday is next month. Is there a very special present I can get for you?"

He shook his head. "I can't think of anything I want, except maybe some peace and quiet. Peace would be the best thing."

He picked up the newspaper and turned past the picture of Aunt Rose and Aunt Lolly. He sighed. "I fear there will not be much peace for anyone, however. There is such disturbing news from Europe. I voted for Woodrow Wilson because he promised to keep us out of war. He told us that American boys would not be sent to fight on European soil. I hope he can keep his promise."

Papa said nothing more, but she could guess what he was thinking. It came as a dreadful shock. She wondered if he still thought of Ben and Nick as little boys, too, but knew in his heart how fast they were growing into young men. Young men were always the ones who were sent away to fight in wars. Suddenly, Bernie was frightened for her brothers. Although she set that terrible thought aside for the moment, she determined from now on to be nicer to them.

Bernie wanted to offer a word of comfort to her father. She remembered some of those voices that had been raised at the first league meeting Aunt Rose had attended. That had also been the night they planned their march in Washington.

She said, "Lots of people in the Lafayette Franchise League are concerned with peace, too. Maybe if more people work together we can make it happen."

"I hope you are right, Bernie. I pray you are right."

Bernie looked up and saw Mother standing in the doorway. She smiled in their direction.

Bernie was determined to do everything in her power to help bring some peace into Papa's life. However, Papa found very little peace and quiet as he read his newspapers. Bernie thought there was a decided increase in him rustling pages. He seemed to be clearing his throat more often. He was especially upset about news of American merchant marine ships being sunk by German U-boats.

Apparently Papa was not the only one in town upset by the news reports. One afternoon, as Bernie walked home from school, she happened to see Edna Schmidt's granddaughter sitting on a curbstone, crying bitterly. Bernie paused and knelt beside the child. She put her arm around the little girl and asked what was wrong.

On May 7, 1915, a German submarine (called a U-boat) torpedoed and sunk the British passenger ship, Lusitania. *Nearly all of the 2,000 passengers perished, including at least 123 Americans. Germany agreed to suspend bombing of passenger ships and merchant vessels in May 1916, but in February the following year it reinstated its policy of unrestricted submarine warfare. Germany sank many U.S. ships in the coming months.*

"They threw rocks at me," Angelina wailed.

Bernie looked around and didn't see anyone. "Who threw rocks at you?"

"Some big boys. Then they ran away."

"Why would they throw rocks at you?"

Angelina sniffed and said haltingly between hiccups, "They said my grandfather is a dirty Hun."

Bernie dried the child's eyes with her handkerchief. "Come with me," she said as she lifted the little girl onto her feet and took her hand.

She led the child two blocks to Graeber's Soda Shop. Inside she helped Angelina climb up onto a stool and asked, "What kind of ice cream would make you feel better?"

"Strawberry." As Angelina licked at her cone, she continued to whimper softly.

Mr. Graeber asked sympathetically, "What makes the child cry so?"

Bernie signaled that he should move further down the counter out of the little girl's hearing.

Bernie whispered, "Some boys threw rocks at her because they said her grandfather is a Hun. She has no idea what that word means."

Mr. Graeber's eyes narrowed into angry slits. "So, this is what it will be like for those of us who have a German name," he said. This war that is surely coming will bring on terrible casualties. Casualties of the body as well as of the spirit. No one will be safe. Even little children will have to suffer."

"I know a lot of people in this town have a bad opinion of Mr. Schmidt, but to take it out on a child is not fair," Bernie said.

"It is true, he is a not-so-nice person," Mr. Graeber replied. "But, did you know that Mr. Schmidt did not become a drinking man until after he came home from the Civil War? He was a Union soldier. I read in the papers that he had been awarded a medal for bravery. Who knows what happened during the war that changed him into what he has become? And so, these young hoodlums tell themselves they are heroes because they throw rocks at his little granddaughter. They tell her that he is a dirty Hun—a German."

Mr. Graeber shook his head. Bernie didn't know if it was more in disgust or sorrow. He turned and walked slowly back into the storeroom at the rear of his shop.

Bernie went back and sat on the stool beside Angelina until the child finished her ice cream. Bernie wiped the remains of it from the little girl's face. Then she took Angelina's hand in hers and walked her home.

12

March Roars Out Like A Lion

Bernie got only as far as the front entryway before her father burst out of the kitchen and saw her. She had tried to be very quiet so that he would not hear her leave the house this evening. He had been trying to read the evening edition of a newspaper, and he still held one dripping page in his hand. The entire paper was still a soggy mess, despite the best efforts of Bernie and her mother. They had opened it up and spread the pages out all over the kitchen. Every flat surface, including the chairs, was covered with papers. The oven had been lit and the door opened in an attempt to hurry the drying process.

Bernie didn't know which made Papa more agitated, the soggy paper or the distressing news that filled every edition lately. Or, he might have been upset by the fact that today's weather had suddenly turned very unpleasant. An electrical storm had caused the street car, which he usually rode to and from work, to be shut down for the day. This meant splashing all the way home from the store in a fierce downpour. His shoes were soaked, and he was sneezing.

As he walked home, the wind had caught the underside of his umbrella and turned it inside out. Two of the ribs were broken, and it collapsed. The poor bedraggled mess was now lying by the front door where he had tossed it in disgust. Without an umbrella he and his newspaper were both soaked by the miserable, sleety, late March rain.

Bernie could not help but think that if only Mother knew how to drive the auto, she could have gone to get him. But of course, Mother did not know how to drive. Papa saw no need for any woman to drive an automobile.

Knowing all of this and understanding full well that Papa still did not approve of her attending the Lafayette Franchise League meetings, Bernie had tiptoed around getting ready to go to the courthouse this evening. She knew

ORIGINAL

SENATE BILL No. 77

A bill for an Act Granting women the right to vote for presidential electors & certain other officers & to vote in certain elections

INTRODUCED BY

Senators Maston and McKinley

1-16 1917, read first time and referred to Committee on Rights Privileges

2-2 1917, reported favorably
Called from Committee on Motion of Senator Maston. Motion of Senator VanAuken to re-commit lost
2-7 Read second time amended & passed to Engrossment

Wm. B. Burford, Printer, Indianapolis.

In February 1917 the Indiana General Assembly passed the Maston–McKinley Bill, also known as the "Partial Suffrage Act," designed to give Indiana women the legal right to vote for "presidential electors, members of [U.S.] Congress, for all statutory officers and on questions except constitutional amendments." Hoosier women around the state registered to vote, and many of them learned about citizenship, the U.S. and state constitutions, voting procedures, and other important topics at meetings such as the one held at the Lafayette Franchise League. However, the law was declared unconstitutional by the Indiana Supreme Court in October of the same year.

that going would only make him more upset. However, despite her best efforts at evasion, Papa caught her at the bottom of the hall stairs.

"What do you think you are doing?" Papa demanded. "Nobody has any business being out on a night like this. I want you to stay home."

"But, Papa, there is a very special meeting tonight. I cannot miss this meeting for the world," Bernie pleaded. How could she make him understand that she needed to be part of this historic gathering?

Papa wanted to know what made tonight so special.

"The meeting is for women to come together so they can learn how to vote."

"Why would you need to learn how to vote?" he muttered. "You are only fourteen years of age."

She could not take the time to explain this to him. "I've got to hurry, Papa. Aunt Lolly will be here for me soon in her auto."

"You would be better off staying home and doing your homework. You're spending far too much of your time at that suffrage league."

Bernie was spared the need to plead any further when Mother came to the kitchen door. "Dear, I think there are a few more pages dry enough for you to read. Do come and sit down. I'll make a cup of hot tea for you."

Papa stomped out of the room and back into the kitchen. Bernie fled through the front door before he could stop her.

The courthouse room where the meeting was scheduled to take place was packed when Bernie, Aunt Rose, Alice, Lizzie, and Aunt Lolly arrived. Despite the terrible weather, women had come out in large groups. Everyone was trying to find a place to sit. An announcement was made that a bigger room would be opened, and the meeting would be moved. Aunt Lolly led the way and they managed to find seats together. More people continued to arrive. Before long, every seat was filled. A side room had to be opened to take care of the overflow.

Aunt Lolly said, "If men are still under the delusion that women are not interested in being able to vote, this turnout ought to change their minds."

Bernie was surprised at all the people she saw there. There were some she knew from the league meetings, but there were as many or more who were unfamiliar. Aunt Lolly and Aunt Rose pointed out that the crowd was made up of women from all walks of life. High society women were there as well as many others. Some were mothers of Bernie's school friends who stayed home to run the household during the day. Several attendees were teachers. There was a woman who worked in the ladies department of Papa's store. There were women who cleaned houses for other women. Some tended to the children of women who spent their time at volunteer work and literary meetings. Even Edna Schmidt and Emily Kennedy had come out in this drenching downpour.

When the clock struck seven, Bernie felt a tremor of excitement. There was an expectant hush as the full import of the moment swept over the crowded courtrooms. She was certain it was a moment all of them would remember for the rest of their lives.

At last, the meeting was called to order. A public official named Mr. Dumfries began to explain the voting procedures. He told them when and where they would vote. Many of the women took notes. Several of them asked questions. When he said that women's votes would have to be kept in separate ballot boxes from those of the men, there was a disquieting buzz from the audience.

"What is the reason for that?" one of the women called out from the back.

"It is because there are thousands of women in this county who are eligible to vote. First, we do not want an important election to be considered void if the Indiana Supreme Court decides that it is, after all, unconstitutional for the women of Indiana to vote. Second, since women have only been given partial suffrage, all offices up for election will not be included on women's ballots."

Aunt Lolly whispered, "I guess the battle is not over yet."

Mr. Dumfries said, "Unless anyone else has a question, that takes care of the official business."

A woman who had been seated near the front of the hall stood. "Before you leave, I would like to tell you a true story and then I am going to make a proposal." She put on eyeglasses in order to read from a paper she held. It rustled in her shaking hands. Her voice was quavering at first, but gained strength as she continued to read.

"More than twenty years ago, Helen Gougar, a well-known woman in our city, decided to take her stand for women's rights. On election day, she went to the polling place. She asked the man in charge for a ballot. When he refused to give one to her, she demanded to know why she was denied the right to vote, stating, 'I am a citizen of the United States of America.'

"The official answered, 'We cannot give you a ballot because you are not a legal voter, being a woman.'"

The woman reading her paper paused and took a deep breath before she said, "Therefore, I think it is only right that the same man, who once denied the vote to that esteemed and well-educated woman, should be named elections inspector. He should be assigned to the very same precinct where this outrage was committed. Let him be the one who now has to hand out ballots to women. He must let them do what that good woman was prevented from doing. Then justice will truly have been done."

Women's voices began to call out, "Yes! Yes! Yes!"

The audience began to sing, "Glory, Glory Hallelujah." Bernie wondered what Papa and Mother would have thought if they could have heard that.

TIPPECANOE COUNTY HISTORICAL ASSOCIATION COLLECTIONS, LAFAYETTE, INDIANA

Helen Gougar (1843–1907) was a suffragist and the first female lawyer in Lafayette, Indiana. Gougar had planned her attempt to vote with the election board in November 1894. Her attempt was done as a means to test the constitutionality of the voting laws. She was denied a ballot and subsequently sued and took her case to court.

SEEIN' IS BELIEVIN'—HAVE A LOOK!

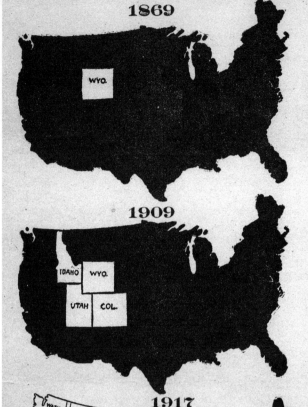

1869

1869

In 1869 the infant territory of Wyoming was the first country in the world to give Suffrage to women on equal terms with men.

1909

1909

In 1909, four states, totaling exactly 17 votes in the Electoral College, represented the fruits of 61 years of agitation for woman suffrage.

1917

1917

Twelve states have Suffrage for women on equal terms with men.

Six other states have Presidential Suffrage for women, and in one additional state women vote in the primaries.

These states control 193 electoral votes.

NATIONAL WOMAN SUFFRAGE PUBLISHING COMPANY, INC.

171 Madison Avenue   Printed February, 1918   New York City

These maps from 1869, 1909, and 1917 show the expansion of women's suffrage over a nearly fifty-year period. Notice the question mark under Indiana's suffrage date. Even though Indiana's General Assembly passed a partial suffrage bill and Governor James P. Goodrich signed it into law, the law was declared unconstitutional by the Indiana Supreme Court.

Mr. Dumfries closed the meeting, stating, "Some men say that a woman's place is in the home and not in the voting booth. I strongly suggest to all the women here tonight to get their spring cleaning done early. That way the diligent housewife can reply that it is all right for her to be there and vote because her housework is all done."

Mr. Dumfries paused. Was he waiting for laughter? Bernie thought he looked overly pleased by his pitiful attempt at humor. Perhaps he thought he would get a round of applause. What he got, instead, was stony silence.

After a moment, a woman's loud voice uttered an indignant, "Humpf!"

Bernie wanted to turn and see who it was but dared not. Then, the woman continued in clear resounding tones, "I have never heard of any man being told his place was at his job and not in the voting booth. No one tells a man he cannot vote until his work is done at his store or in his office. I have never heard of a farmer being told he could not engage in politics until his crops were all in. Yet you, sir, think it is amusing to tell women to get their housework done before they vote."

Applause began as a ripple and then became a roar like the rolling thunder outside the building. Mr. Dumfries stood with his mouth open, his ears glowing red in embarrassment, and then he turned to make his escape from the meeting in a hurry. Mr. Dumfries got his applause all right, but not the way he expected.

On the way home, Bernie said to Aunt Lolly, "Well, I guess we have won at last, haven't we?"

"What do you mean?"

"I mean that women in Indiana, Illinois, New York, and I forget how many other states now have the vote. There's nothing left for us to do."

"As a matter of fact," Aunt Lolly said, "it means that we shall have to work all the harder until all our sisters in every state can vote. Women's right to vote must become a part of the U.S. Constitution. Plus, in Indiana we still can't vote for all elected offices. We only received partial suffrage under the bill that was passed. This means we still can't vote for governor, secretary of state, state treasurer, U.S. senators or representatives, or to ratify constitutional amendments."

The storm was still raging when Bernie arrived home after the meeting. She saw Papa sitting in the parlor in the dark. He had waited up for her. When she entered, he said, "I see you are home safely." Then he went upstairs without another word. He seemed to be carrying a heavy load.

via Galveston

JAN 19 1917

GERMAN LEGATION

MEXICO CITY

130	13042	13401	8501	115	3528	416	17214	6491	11310
18147	18222	21560	10247	11518	23677	13605	3494	14936	
98092	5905	11311	10392	10371	0302	21290	5161	39695	
23571	17504	11269	18276	18101	0317	0228	17694	4473	
23284	22200	19452	21589	67893	5569	13918	8958	12137	
1333	4725	4458	5905	17166	13851	4458	17149	14471	6706
13850	12224	6929	14991	7382	15857	67893	14218	36477	
5870	17553	67893	5870	5454	16102	15217	22801	17138	
21001	17388	7446	23638	18222	6719	14331	15021	23845	
3156	23552	22096	21604	4797	9497	22464	20855	4377	
23610	18140	22260	5905	13347	20420	39689	13732	20667	
6929	5275	18507	52262	1340	22049	13339	11265	22295	
10439	14814	4178	6992	8784	7632	7357	6926	52262	11267
21100	21272	9346	9559	22464	15874	18502	18500	15857	
2188	5376	7381	98092	16127	13486	9350	9220	76036	14219
5144	2831	17920	11347	17142	11264	7667	7762	15099	9110
10482	97556	3569	3670						

BEPNSTOPFF.

Charge German Embassy.

The Zimmermann Telegram was sent in code from German Foreign Minister Arthur Zimmermann to the German Minister to Mexico in January 1917. British cryptographers, people who make and break codes, decoded this telegram and sent it to U.S. President Woodrow Wilson in late February. The telegram recommended an alliance between Mexico and Germany against the United States. If successful, Germany promised to give Mexico the parts of the United States that Mexico had lost in the Mexican–American War: Texas, New Mexico, and Arizona. The Zimmermann Telegram helped draw the United States into war with Germany.

After all of the evening's excitement, Bernie found it hard to sleep that night. She crept down to the kitchen to make a cup of warm cocoa. A few remaining pages of Papa's damp newspaper were spread over the table and chairs drying out. As she waited for the milk to heat, Bernie glanced at the headlines. Papa was right to be concerned. The czar of Russia and his family had been exiled to Siberia by revolutionaries. Ireland was in turmoil with its own revolution against England. The German government was trying to convince Mexico to rise up against the United States. In exchange for its cooperation, Germany was promising to return some of America's southwest territory to Mexico. No wonder Papa had been in such a mood!

As Bernie drank her cocoa, she read a brief article with a bold headline:

April is the Month of War
Superstitious people, and some who are not superstitious but merely observing, are pointing to the fact that with the exception of the war with England in 1812, foreign wars in which the United States has been involved, started during the month of April. The War of the Revolution began April 19, 1775, at Concord and Lexington. The War with Mexico began April 24, 1846. War was declared against Spain April 21, 1898. Now in order to add force to this statement, let it be considered that the civil war began with the Fort Sumpter attack April 12, 1861, and the Black Hawk war, the greatest conflict with Indian forces, began April 21, 1831. The first of April is at hand. —

A chilly shiver ran down Bernie's back. She pulled her flannel dressing gown closer around her. Bernie had no idea how all of this was going to affect her family, but somehow she was certain it would. She crept back up to her room to try to sleep as the storm shook the world outside her window.

13

Dark Clouds Gather

The storm that had raged so ominously outside a few days earlier seemed to have moved inside the Epperson home. All of Papa's worst fears hovered like dark clouds, and each family member reacted in a different way.

Since the April 6th declaration of war against Germany by the U.S. Congress, Papa now shook his newspaper more fiercely as he read it. Often, he would also explode in disgust, "How can people be so blind? When the British got into this war in 1914, they said it would be over by Christmas. Now here we are, three years later, repeating the same idiotic thing! Don't we learn anything from the past?"

When Papa, usually so calm, railed out like this, Mother would jump up from the table and hurry to the kitchen with frantic little cries. "Your eggs are getting cold. Do you want me to warm up your coffee? Here, have some of the good raspberry jam I made last summer." Sometimes Bernie wondered if her mother thought all the world's problems could be put right with food.

Bernie, on the other hand, viewed this as a wonderful opportunity to prove to Papa how important it was for women to get the vote. One morning at the breakfast table she managed to get part of Papa's newspaper and started to read aloud from an article that she thought proved her point. "It says here that not all members of our Congress voted to declare war. 'Representative Jeannette Rankin of Montana voted No. She was only one of a few representatives who voted not to send American men to fight in Europe. She was the only woman in Congress, but she rose from her seat and proclaimed bravely, 'I want to stand by my country, but I cannot vote for war.'"

After Bernie read the newspaper article, she commented, "If all the women in this country were able to vote, maybe we wouldn't be in a war."

She glared at Ben and Nick, practically daring them to make their usual smart-alecky comments. To her surprise, neither of her brothers said anything. Nick only snorted and shrugged his shoulders. Ben, who would be a high school graduate in less than two months, just kept eating as he stared past her with a distant look in his eyes.

Later, Bernie was even more surprised that not all suffragists applauded Rankin's opposition to the war. Some said that anyone who disagreed with the war was unpatriotic. Most of those in the Lafayette Franchise League insisted that it was their duty as citizens to put aside the cause of women's rights until after the war ended.

Even though Nick had not said anything to Bernie after she read the article about Jeannette Rankin, she discovered later that he wholeheartedly disagreed with her position. He said to her, out of Papa's hearing, that he fervently hoped the war would not be over by Christmas. He had always wanted to be a soldier. One day she heard him singing, in an off-key voice, the popular song written by George M. Cohan, "Over There." Nick's raspy tones boomed out when he got to the words, "The Yanks are coming, and we won't be back till it's over, over there."

She countered by shoving a newspaper clipping under the door of his room. The article told the sad story of the eighteen-year-old son of British writer Rudyard Kipling who had been killed on his first day in battle. Bernie added a handwritten note in the margin of the piece, "War is not the glorious adventure you think it is."

Nick did not bother to respond to her warning. Usually he delighted in arguing with her. She was dismayed that he would not take the time to discuss the war with her. She was even more upset when she discovered that he kept a large map of the world posted on the wall of his bedroom. She saw that he had marked every battle location with a pinhead of a different color. He had saved a large stack of articles about these battles, which he clipped from the newspapers after Papa had discarded them. When he caught her in his room one day looking at the map, he reacted very strangely. Instead of accusing her of being snoopy, he did not say a word. He merely grinned in a most puzzling way as she brushed past him to leave the room.

If Nick was elated by the prospect of war, Bernie was distressed by the fact that everything seemed to change overnight, especially things Bernie thought were vitally important. The suffragists still wanted to get a constitutional amendment passed so that all women in the United States could vote, but that appeared to have taken a back seat to the war effort. It seemed to Bernie that all they did now during their league meetings was talk about what they could do to help the men in the army.

One of the members reported about a group of Indiana women who wrote letters to soldiers to help keep up their morale. "It is very important for men away from home to get mail. Not every soldier has someone to write to him. Think how terrible it must feel to be left out at mail call," she said.

The letter writers were from Henry County, Indiana, from a group called the "Sammy Girls." Bernie wondered if this clever name was adopted because of the recruitment poster that showed an older, bearded man wearing a top hat, pointing outward, stating, "Uncle Sam Wants You."

It was proposed and immediately seconded that the league would encourage their members to correspond with soldiers. Letter writing became something of a competition among the women. Everyone tried to see who could write the most. A tally board was displayed at meetings. It was dutifully filled

Jeannette Rankin of Montana was the first female member of Congress. She advocated for the creation of a committee on women's suffrage, and when the committee was created she was appointed one of its members. In January 1918 she opened the first House floor debate about a constitutional amendment on women's suffrage. Rankin left Congress in 1918 but returned in 1940. She was the only Congressional Representative to vote against U.S. entry into both world wars.

in as members responded to the roll call with the number of letters they had written during the past month.

Groups of women also met to knit socks, scarves, and other useful items to send to the soldiers. Even Aunt Rose put aside her crocheted doilies and began to knit grey-green colored sweaters to send to the boys on the front in France. Other women gathered to tear bed sheets into long strips and roll them into surgical dressings for the wounded.

One league member heard that pits from peaches and other fruits as well as some nut shells and seeds were needed to make filters in gas masks, so the women started bringing in containers of pits to the meetings. It took quite a while for the league to discover where these pits should be sent. Lizzie told Bernie that Uncle Leroy was spending every evening in his barn workshop trying to invent a better gas mask to protect the soldiers.

Germany introduced chemical warfare in 1915 with chlorine gas. That same year Hoosier chemist James Bert Garner discovered that poisonous chemicals could be neutralized with activated charcoal made from natural fibers found in peach pits and other fruit pits and in some seeds, nuts, and nut shells. Americans gathered pits, nuts, and shells and sent them to the Red Cross so that they could be used in gas masks such as the one shown here. These masks saved numerous lives on the battlefield. Garner earned bachelor's and master's degrees from Wabash College in Crawfordsville, Indiana, and was head of the chemistry department there from 1901 to 1914.

Bernie knew that there were women in the league who had wanted to work for peace. Where were they now? Even she had given up. Writing editorials about peace seemed of no avail since the United States had entered the war. What could she do to make a difference?

Try as she might, she simply could not learn how to knit. Aunt Rose gave up trying to teach her. She began skipping league meetings despite Alice's and Lizzie's best efforts to encourage her to attend.

Bernie remembered what Mr. Graeber had said about war and the suffering it would bring. But what could anyone do about it now? It seemed as though once the war epidemic struck, everyone came down with it. Bernie did not want to think about it. Her mood seemed as dark as Papa's.

14

Nick Disappears

It was Bernie who found the note on a Sunday afternoon in late September. She had a report due the next day for her tenth grade history class, and she needed her dictionary to find out if she should use the word "emigrate" or "immigrate."

"Mother, I can't find my dictionary."

"Do you suppose one of the boys has it?"

She went back upstairs and knocked on Ben's door. "Have you seen my dictionary?"

He was bent over his college chemistry text. "I don't have it. Ask Nick."

"He's not in his room."

"He should be back before long from his camping trip with Jack."

"I need my dictionary right now. Maybe he borrowed it and took it without asking me. I'm going to look in his room."

"Watch out for booby traps or green monsters." Ben was joking, but he wasn't far off the mark.

Bernie hated going into either of the boys' rooms. She never knew what she was going to find, especially in Nick's. It was a gloomy day, so she turned on the light. To her great surprise she did not have to step over the usual piles of dirty clothes strewn about. She went to the shelf under the window. It held a tattered collection of dime novels—those awful paperback books that Mother did not want him to read. She noticed a glass jar full of colorful marbles. She wrinkled up her nose at the wad of chewed gum stuck on the lid. A couple of stubby pencils, a scruffy pad of paper, and a slingshot lay atop his algebra book. There was no sign of her dictionary.

Bernie decided to look under the bed, bringing up a memory of another day long ago. Mother had sent her upstairs to collect Nick's dirty clothes for the laundry. She had found a box under the bed. When she had lifted the lid to peek inside, three frogs had leaped out. Bernie had run shrieking from the room. After that, the boys always teased her about the green monsters. Mother was not at all happy about having frogs hopping about upstairs. Papa laughed it off with the usual, "Boys will be boys."

Bernie also noticed that Nick's bed was not the usual tangled mess of covers. It was neatly made and smoothed out. She got down on her knees and lifted the spread so that she could look beneath it. Another surprise. There was nothing under the bed, not even the balls of dust that she expected to find. She stood up, put her hands on her hips, and wondered what in the world he would have done with it. He had to have her dictionary. She had looked all over the house. Where else could it be? There was nothing to do but wait until he got home and confront him. Then she saw her dictionary lying on the small table at the far side of the bed. She picked it up and noticed something tucked inside its pages. At first she thought it might be his homework, but it was not. It was an envelope addressed to "My Family."

Bernie held the envelope in her hands and stared at it for a moment. The writing was Nick's, but it was very neat and not his usual scrawl. It looked as though he had taken a lot of effort with it. She started to open it, but something about it made her change her mind. She took it downstairs and handed it to Papa.

"I found this in Nick's room. I thought you ought to see it."

Papa looked at her and then at the envelope with a puzzled expression. Carefully he opened it and withdrew a single page, which he read to himself. Then he read it again.

Mother was sewing a button on Papa's shirt and glanced up before she went back to her sewing.

Papa inhaled sharply, leaned his head back, and closed his eyes.

"What is it?" Mother asked. "Are you all right?"

"Nick has run away," he said slowly.

"That can't be right. Why would he do such a thing?"

Papa handed her the note. Mother started to read it aloud but got no farther than, "Dear Mother and Father. Please don't be upset." She broke down sobbing and let the note fall to the floor. Papa got up out of his easy chair. He went over to her and put his arms around her.

During World War I, posters were a major propaganda tool the military used to recruit men, build support for the war, and call on those at home to send supplies from home to the war zones. Many messages on recruiting posters appealed to people's sense of duty, honor, responsibility, and patriotism. Nick likely would have seen posters such as this one, and they would have influenced his decision to enlist.

"Now, now, calm down, my dear. Everything will be all right. I'll take care of this."

Bernie picked up the note and read the rest of it to herself.

Jack and I have gone to join the army. You know that this is what I have always wanted to do. People say the war will be over by Christmas, so I've got to go right away because I don't want to miss out. President Wilson says that this is a war to make the world safe for democracy. I love my family. I love my country. I want to serve it like Uncle Charley did. Please try to understand.
Nick

"That fool!" Papa exploded. At first, Bernie thought he was talking about Nick until Papa said, "That crazy old fool. Uncle Charley and all his made-up stories about being a soldier in the Civil War."

Ben heard the uproar and came downstairs. "What's going on down here?"

Bernie handed him Nick's note. He read it, then said, "I don't believe it. Jack wouldn't run off and join the army. There's no way he would leave his sister and her children without him there to protect them from Mr. McClarty."

Bernie said, "Didn't you know? His sister is not there anymore. Aunt Lolly helped Emily and her little ones move out. She found a place for Jack's sister to stay and work. They're living with a family and Emily is working as their housekeeper."

"When did that happen?"

"Three or four days ago. It was just before Jack and Nick left for their camping trip."

Mother was weeping hysterically. Papa helped her to lie down. He put an afghan over her knees. She kept moaning, "We've got to get him back."

"Bernie, get your mother a drink of water," he said.

When she came back from the kitchen, Papa was pacing across the parlor floor.

"What are we going to do? He's only sixteen!" Mother repeated.

"I know the army recruiter here in town. I'll call him," Papa said and went to the telephone in the kitchen.

When he came back, Papa said, "The recruiter hasn't heard anything about this. He hasn't seen either boy. He thinks they were too smart to try to enlist here where everyone knows them."

Mother started to cry again. Papa sat beside her and patted her arm reassuringly.

"I'll get on the interurban and go to Indianapolis first thing tomorrow morning. I have connections with some people down there who may be able to help. Nick is too young to join the army. I'm sure we can get him sent back home."

"Come on," Papa told Mother. "I am going to help you go upstairs. I want you to get into bed. You need to rest."

He turned to Ben and said, "Call the doctor and tell him your mother needs something to help her sleep."

COURTESY OF MARY BLAIR IMMEL

This underage World War I soldier enlisted at age fifteen. His discharge papers show that he was sent to France and was in some of the worst battles of the war. His older brother, who was also a soldier in the First World War, went to Fort Harrison in Indianapolis where he almost died of influenza.

Bernie didn't know what to do. After Ben had placed the call, the two of them sat in the darkening gloom of the parlor.

"What are we going to do?" she asked.

Ben answered, "Papa will take care of it, but we probably ought to pray that Papa doesn't kill Uncle Charley."

"What did Papa mean when he said Uncle Charley made up all those stories about being in the Civil War?" Bernie asked.

"I suppose he meant that Uncle Charley was never a soldier. It was actually his brother, our Grandpa Mifflin, who was in the Civil War. Of course, Grandpa never talked about it, but I once saw a carte de visite of him in his uniform."

"A card—what?" Bernie asked.

"A carte de visite," Ben explained. "It's an old-fashioned kind of picture. A lot of soldiers had them made when they first went into the army."

"Why would Uncle Charley say that he was in the Union Army if he wasn't?" Bernie wondered.

"From what I have heard, Uncle Charley was too young to go to war, but he liked hanging around the old soldiers who used to sit on the benches outside the courthouse. He listened to their stories and later, he passed them off for his own. So, when Nick was a very little boy, Uncle Charley told him those stories. The wider Nick's eyes became, the more exciting the stories became. I suppose he liked being Nick's favorite uncle. None of us thought it would ever come to this."

Bernie realized that Aunt Rose had hinted about this on the train, but she had never come right out and accused Uncle Charley of not telling the truth. She felt angry and left out.

"Why didn't anyone tell me?"

"I guess no one thought it was important," Ben answered. "You were just a little girl and nobody thought you would pay any attention to a bunch of made-up war stories."

"But someone should have told Nick the truth. Why didn't you straighten him out?"

"Well, back then we didn't know there was going to be a war, did we?" Ben said. "Nobody thought he'd have a chance to pull a dumb stunt like this."

15

Mother's Secret

It was now two weeks since Nick and Jack had run away to join the army. Mother was still having a difficult time accepting the fact that the boys were gone. Aunt Rose and Aunt Lolly took turns coming over to stay with her every weekday until Bernie came home from school.

Papa didn't want Mother left alone. She had hardly stopped crying since he returned from Indianapolis after his unsuccessful attempt to find the boys. The recruiter there had told him that he could not locate anyone in the enrollment lists named Nick Epperson or Jack McClarty. He suggested that they had changed their names when they signed up. It was not uncommon.

Papa had insisted that someone should have realized that Nick was too young to join the army. He was told that if an enlistee swore he was old enough, no one had the time to check and see if it was true. Nick certainly wouldn't be the first underage boy to lie about how old he was. The boys probably vouched for each other. The recruiters had quotas to meet. The boys would probably get in touch with their parents one of these days. All they could do was wait for a letter.

Bernie hurried home from school. She stepped inside the front hallway and called, "Aunt Rose?" There was no answer. "Aunt Lolly? Anybody?" Still no response.

Bernie climbed the stairs and dropped her schoolbooks on the desk in her room. She walked across the hall to her parents' room. The door was open and she could see that the curtains had been pulled open and fastened to let in the sunlight. Mother was not lying on the bed with a cloth over her eyes, as she had done so often lately.

Bernie knocked softly before she stepped tentatively into the room. She still didn't see anyone. "Mother? Where are you? Are you all right?"

"I'm here. Come in, dear."

Bernie looked about the room. She was surprised to see her mother sitting on the floor at the far side of the bed. There was a small trunk open nearby.

"Come here and sit beside me," Mother said. "There are some things I want you to see."

Bernie waited as Mother lifted various items out of the trunk and placed them on the floor. At last, she found what she was looking for. She handed it to Bernie. It was a theatrical playbill. The date on it was June 3, 1896.

Bernie was puzzled. "What is this all about?"

"Look at it carefully," Mother said.

Bernie read the words aloud: "The New Touring Players Proudly Present: 'Midnight in the Sheik's Harem.'" The drama was described as "a thrilling account of an escape from a fate worse than death."

Bernie was still puzzled, but Mother did not say anything. Bernie read on, looking at the list of cast members. Near the bottom she saw: "Fatima—A beautiful damsel in distress played by Melisande Mifflin."

Mifflin! That was Mother's last name before she and Papa were married, but who in the world was Melisande?

"Is she a relative of ours?" Bernie asked. "I've never heard of her."

"Perhaps you can you guess?" Mother smiled a strange little smile and Bernie saw her mother's cheeks turn a rosy color.

"Not you?"

Mother nodded.

"Where was this play performed?"

"It was presented in several different towns. You will notice that the acting company was called 'The New Touring Players.'"

"How did you get to be a part of this?" Bernie stared at the play program and could hardly believe what she was seeing.

"I suppose that my love for the dramatic started in school. I always won prizes for recitation. It was exciting to be the center of attention." Mother removed the lid of another box she held on her lap. It was full of ribbons and rosettes, certificates, and two small silver trophies.

"Did you win all of these?"

Mother nodded. "People told me how much talent I had. I began to dream that I could become an actress. The summer I was nineteen, a theatrical company came to town. They advertised in the newspaper that they needed townspeople to act as background crowd for their production. I auditioned and showed the manager my awards. He said I was perfect. I appeared on the stage for the next few nights while the company was in town. On the final night of the production, the manager said that they had a small part for me in a play. He asked if I would like to travel with them. I was thrilled and foolishly said that I would love to go."

"Secretly, I packed a bag and went with them. I left a note telling my parents what I had done, but not who I was with. It wasn't hard for them to figure out, because they knew I had gone three nights in a row to the theater. They didn't know what to do, but your Uncle Leroy said he would find me. When he heard about it, Edward—your Papa—insisted that he would go along. Of course, he wasn't your father then. We weren't even engaged to be married."

COURTESY OF MARY BLAIR IMMEL

This photo, ca. 1917, depicts a girl wearing an outfit that Bernie might have worn to school: a middy blouse, dark skirt, and long black stockings with sturdy leather shoes.

Bernie sat and stared at her mother as she spoke. She simply could not imagine her doing such a thing. "But why is your name listed as Melisande Mifflin in the play program?"

"I thought it was a beautiful and romantic name. If I was going to be an actress, I needed a name more dramatic than my own. Martha Jane Mifflin seemed far too plain for an actress."

Mother continued, "I was gone almost three weeks before Leroy and Edward managed to track the company by following the newspaper announcements and billboards. They went to each town

Traveling theater companies, such as this one out of Mankato, Minnesota, stopped at many rural communities throughout the United States, bringing much-needed entertainment to the people who lived there. Bernie's mother joined a group similar to this.

where the New Touring Players had appeared. One night Leroy and Edward showed up at the stage door of a theater in Peoria, Illinois. They demanded to see me. At first the doorman claimed they had never heard of me, but Edward insisted that he and my brother be allowed to go inside for a look around. When they found me, they took me home. At first the doorman would not allow me to take my belongings. He said I owed the company money for my lodging and food."

"Do you mean you had to leave your clothing and everything?"

"I would have if Edward hadn't looked the man straight in the eye and threatened to call the police if they did not return my things. He was very forceful. The doorman seemed to wilt and got my things immediately. I can tell you that it was much more dramatic than anything I had seen on the stage."

"Were you upset when Uncle Leroy and Papa forced you to come back home with them?"

"Oh, my goodness, no. I was never so happy to see anyone in my life," Mother said. She fished a handkerchief out of her pocket and dabbed at her overflowing eyes. It was a few minutes before she was able to continue.

"You see, I found out the hard way that show business wasn't the lovely, glamorous dream I imagined it would be. Oh, yes, I had my name printed in the program, but I only appeared on stage to carry a tray or announce a visitor. A few times I got to scream and then faint on a couch. I never had many lines to say. My costume was tacky and smelled so awful I could barely stand to put it on. I tried not to think who had worn it last. I don't think it had ever been washed. Most of the time I ran errands for the real actors and actresses. I did whatever anyone told me. Sew this button on, find my hat, go get this and go get that. And they didn't always tell me in a nice manner."

"Why didn't you try to get away from them?"

"I couldn't. I didn't have any money. I quickly spent what little I brought with me. The manager had promised to pay me but he never did. He always had some excuse. We moved from town to town continually. Half the time I wasn't even sure exactly where we were. We stayed in terrible run-down boarding houses with dirty sheets. Once I got out of bed in the middle of the night and stepped on something that crackled unpleasantly under foot." Mother wrinkled her nose and shivered at the memory. "It was a cockroach. One time we even had to sneak out during the night because the manager said our last performance hadn't earned enough money to pay the hotel bill."

"Why didn't you go to the police and tell them you needed help?"

"I suppose I was afraid to have my family find out what a terrible mess I had gotten myself into."

Bernie cringed as she tried to imagine her mother as a frightened young woman.

"I was surprised that Edward came after me. I was even more surprised when he said he wanted to marry me. The whole thing was a bit of a scandal in town. I learned later that his parents ordered him to break off the engagement. They wanted him to have nothing to do with that 'wild Mifflin girl.' Later, I learned how Edward stood up to them."

Bernie could hardly take in everything that Mother told her.

"Furthermore, he told them he would not be a part of his father's business if they made any trouble about the marriage. He said he would move away and take me with him."

"It's like a novel by Jane Austen or Emily Bronte," Bernie gasped.

Mother laughed softly. "When I think back on it, it seems the same way to me. It is like a story that happened to someone else. When his parents relented and said we could marry, I made a promise to myself that I would be the ideal wife and never cause him any more trouble."

Bernie wondered if that episode explained why Mother was so careful about visiting Grandmother Epperson regularly to keep in her good graces. It might also explain why Mother was always so prim and proper. This must be why she seemed to care so much about what other people thought.

Mother started to weep again, softly. "Now, I feel that I have failed."

"Mother, please don't cry anymore," Bernie pleaded. "It frightens me."

"I can't help it. I keep thinking that maybe it's my fault that Nick ran away."

"How could that be?"

"Because Nick did the same thing I did."

"Papa thinks Nick ran away because of Uncle Charley and all of his boasting about things he never did."

"I can't help but wonder if running away is some trait inherited through the Mifflin family. Maybe his parents were right and Papa should not have married me. Maybe I was not good enough for him."

Bernie leaned close to her mother and hugged her. "Mother, I don't believe that. You must not blame yourself. Nick got carried away by all the excitement. He thinks being a soldier will be a glorious adventure. Remember, the recruiter told Papa that Nick is not the only boy who has ever run off to join the army."

Mother and daughter sat quietly together, each lost in her own thoughts as the afternoon began to fade away. Bernie recalled that Aunt Rose had told her on the train that she was more like her mother than she realized. This must have been what she meant. Of course, she had not run away as her mother had done, although she had gone off to Washington, DC, without revealing the full reason for the trip. Bernie had to admit she was impetuous. Whenever Papa scolded her, he said that she must stop and think ahead about the consequences of her actions. She knew she caused Papa a lot of worry. She remembered the words that Mother had whispered to her when she broke her arm. What was it she had said? Something about the pain of learning lessons the hard way.

Sometimes Bernie felt as though her life was like a gigantic jigsaw puzzle. Little by little, as she put more pieces together, she was seeing a picture of her family emerge that she had not been aware of before.

Written in 1915, "I Didn't Raise My Boy to Be a Soldier" was the first commercially successful anti-war song. It is a mother's lament over the loss of a son and how victory is no consolation.

It seemed odd to think of Papa doing what he did when Mother ran away. He was not just the man who got dressed up each morning, read the newspaper, and went to work. Now, he seemed kind of like a brave knight who had rescued a damsel in distress. He loved that damsel, no matter what foolish thing she had done. And he had stood up to his parents in order to make Martha Jane Mifflin his wife.

Bernie knew that Papa loved her, too, no matter what she did. She made up her mind that she would be a bit more cautious and try to think things through more carefully before she acted. However, she was determined not to let anyone stifle her dreams. But, how could she manage to do both?

PART 3

1918 TO 1920

16

Ben Answers the Call

Papa no longer read the morning newspaper at the breakfast table or settled down with his evening paper in the parlor after supper. In fact, he allowed no papers in the house anymore. Bernie knew that Papa was doing his best to shield Mother from any news about the war. She worried enough about Nick as it was.

Bernie also knew that Papa spent more and more time in his small office at the rear of Epperson's Emporium. It was where he went to read the newspapers. She often stopped in at the store after school for a brief visit with him. He had removed the large map of the world from the wall in Nick's room. It was now installed above his desk at the store. Papa kept track of all war action, just as Nick had done. The number of colored pins increased daily. She supposed he wondered, as she did, if Nick was involved in any of those terrible battles. Nick never wrote letters home, so there was no telling where he was.

One late-March afternoon, Bernie learned that the Germans had begun a major attack and had broken through British lines south of the French town of Arras. When she visited Papa's office, she noticed that there was already a colored pin sticking out of that part of France. Bernie thought that might have been what made him seem especially subdued during the evening meal that night.

Mother, too, was especially quiet and seldom spoke except to ask if anyone wanted more green beans or potatoes. Even Ben seemed far away in a world of his own. Bernie listened to the pendulum of the tall grandfather clock as it swung rhythmically back and forth. It seemed to match the beating of her aching heart. She wished that she could end the silence but could think of nothing to say.

FRANK M. MCMURRY, *THE GEOGRAPHY OF THE GREAT WAR* (NEW YORK: MACMILLAN, 1918), 35.

Though World War I was fought along several different fronts, American soldiers such as Nick were sent to the Western Front, depicted by the bold line on this map, spanning France and Belgium. British and French troops had been fighting German troops along this line since 1914. The Western Front moved very little in the years before the Americans joined the fight. On the ground, it consisted of two sets of deep trenches or ditches, one on the German side of the line, and one on the side occupied by the French, British, and their allies. Hundreds of thousands of young men died violent deaths in these trenches over the course of the war. Many of the survivors suffered illnesses such as trench foot, a fungal disease that could cause rotting of the skin and lead to amputation, due to water collecting in the ditches, where the soldiers were forced to stay.

She did not like the change that had come over their household. Nick had always made them groan with laughter at his clowning around. There were no longer any arguments. She was surprised to find that she missed the teasing she used to endure from her brothers.

When the serving bowls had been passed around a second time, but no one wanted any more to eat, Mother said, "Bernie, you can start clearing things from the table. I'll get the dessert ready."

Mother left the room with a swish of her long dark skirt. It was strange, but Bernie had a premonition that she would always remember that sound. It would forever bring back the memory of what happened that evening, for in the next moment she heard a tone in Ben's voice that filled her with dread.

He said very quietly, "Papa, I need to speak with you privately right after dinner."

Bernie did not eat her dessert but went immediately into the kitchen to start the washing up. As soon as she and Mother had finished in the kitchen, Bernie hurried upstairs before Papa and Ben came up to talk in her brother's room. When she saw that Ben had not closed his door all the way, she positioned herself in the hallway at a point where she could overhear the conversation.

Bernie knew she should not eavesdrop. Mother always warned her that those who listen in on other people's conversations never hear anything good about themselves. This time, however, what she heard was nothing about herself; it was news that sent a cold chill slithering up her spine.

The American military segregated its forces until 1948, so in World War I, whites and African Americans served in separate divisions. The majority of white units, such as the 16th Infantry, 1st Division, participated in some fierce fighting during 1918. While many African American soldiers were relegated to supply jobs, there were African American combat soldiers, as well. The image on the left shows Indiana soldiers from the 16th Infantry. The African American soldier on the right is Les Brown from Indianapolis.

Ben said, "I have something to say, Papa. You are not going to like it, but I have to tell you. And I don't know of any other way than to say it straight out."

"Go ahead, son. Get on with it."

"I am going to quit college and join the army," Ben continued. "A bunch of the fellows at school are signing up tomorrow. We want to go together so that we can be in the same company."

Bernie crept closer so that she could catch a glimpse of the two of them, sitting side by side on the end of Ben's bed. Papa's face drained of color for a moment, then it began to get very red. He stood and the first few words came out as a shout. "How could you do this? You foolish, foolish boy." Then he lowered his voice to say, "It was bad enough when Nick ran off and enlisted. Are you trying to destroy our family? Didn't you give one single thought about what this would do to your mother? She is already sick with worry over your brother."

Bernie held her breath, waiting for Ben to shout back at Papa—but that was not Ben's way. He replied firmly, but quietly, "You know that I would not want to do anything to hurt Mother—or you. But, sometimes a man has to do what a man must do."

Bernie felt both frightened and proud as she looked at Ben, who had risen and stood ramrod straight with his shoulders thrust back defiantly as he faced his angry father. She thought he looked like a soldier already.

"Papa, please try to understand."

"What I understand is that this war has nothing to do with us. It's Europe's business and President Wilson knows that full well. I voted for the man because he promised to keep us out of it. Now look at what has happened." Papa's voice broke with emotion.

Ben continued calmly, "I don't like this war any better than you do, but I feel that I have to go. The other fellows in my class are all going. My younger brother has gone already. How can I stay safely at home? Do you want me to feel unpatriotic or like a coward?"

Papa opened his mouth. Bernie braced herself for another volcanic eruption. But Papa just stood there. Something stopped him from continuing the argument. Bernie thought Papa looked like a man who had just crashed into a brick wall.

She watched in amazement as Papa stepped toward Ben and put his hand on Ben's shoulder. "You take care of yourself, son. I'll watch over your mother. We'll get through this somehow."

Ben stepped forward and put his arms around Papa and hugged him close. For the first time she noticed how much taller Ben was than Papa. It was all Bernie could do to keep from dashing into the room and throwing her arms around the two of them. Papa quickly turned his face away from Ben. Bernie was certain she had seen a tear making its way down Papa's cheek. She had rarely seen her father cry. Bernie hurried back to her room and closed the door quietly so they would not know she had witnessed this scene.

* * *

As it happened, Ben's time in the army did not last long. It was only three months from the time he enlisted that the situation took a drastic turn.

Early that summer, Bernie came home from the library one afternoon to find Aunt Lolly's car parked in front of the house. Inside, Bernie saw Papa

LIBRARY OF CONGRESS, PRINTS AND PHOTOGRAPHS DIVISION, LC-USZ62-41940

By the end of 1914, the year fighting started, more than 6,000 miles of trenches had been dug on either side of the Western Front; the miles of trenches would nearly double by the end of the war. Between the opposing trench lines was "no man's land," where vegetation soon died out with all the shelling and gunfire. No man's land was also filled with sharp barbed wire to slow the advance of attacks.

bounding down the stairs two at a time. That was strange. He never came home from work until six o'clock, just in time for supper. But here he was carrying a suitcase.

He didn't seem to notice Bernie as he stepped into the entryway and called out, "Hurry up. We've got to catch that four o'clock train."

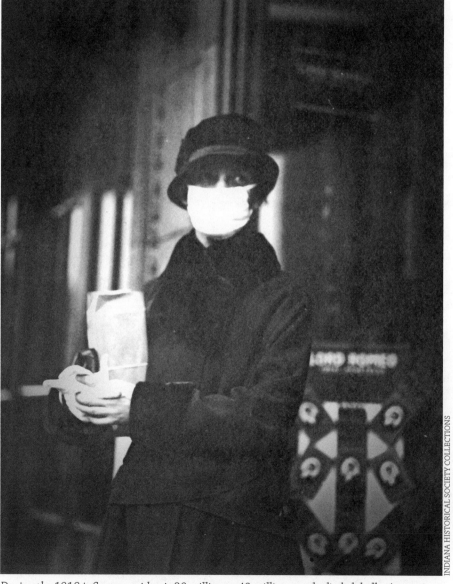

During the 1918 influenza epidemic 20 million to 40 million people died globally. Approximately 43,000 American servicemen died of the flu. In Indiana the deadliest outbreak was from October 1918 through February 1919, killing around 10,000 people.

"She's coming," Aunt Lolly said from where she stood by the railing at the top of the stair. "Come on, Martha. I've got your suitcase."

"I'm just checking to see if I have forgotten anything," Mother said.

"If you don't have it, you'll have to do without," Papa shouted impatiently.

"What's happening?" Bernie asked. "Where are you going?"

Papa thrust a yellow envelope into her hands. "Read this. We're going to Kentucky."

Bernie removed the telegram. "Is this about Nick? Have they found him?"

"No, it's about Ben."

Aunt Lolly herded Mother and Papa out the front door and into her waiting car.

"I'll take your parents to the station and then come back to get you, Bernie. Pack your things," Aunt Lolly shouted as she eased out of her parking spot. "You're going to stay with us at the farm while your parents are gone."

Bernie read the telegram. The brevity of the words made her knees tremble with fear. She reached out to grasp the banister to keep from falling. She read the message again.

"BEN VERY ILL. INFLUENZA. COME IMMEDIATELY." The message was from somebody named Joey at Camp Zachary Taylor. Bernie knew that Camp Taylor was where Ben's company was stationed in Kentucky.

Up until now, Bernie had worried about what might happen to one of her brothers on the battlefield. The possibility of deathly illness had never entered her mind. Of course, she was aware, as was everyone, that there were many people sick with the dreaded disease. Some of her classes had been half empty toward the end of the school year, and there had been talk of closing her school until the illness had passed. Many people wore gauze surgical masks over their nose and mouth when they went out in public. She had read the headlines in the newspaper at Papa's office about the large numbers of people dying. The disease wasn't only in the United States. People all over the world were sick with influenza—it was being called a pandemic.

When Aunt Lolly came back from the train station, she explained further. One of Ben's friends had sent the telegram because he was so worried about Ben. It had arrived at the Emporium only a couple of hours earlier. Papa had made a telephone call to Kentucky to find out what the situation was and then rushed home. Mother had insisted they leave right away.

"I'm not at all certain what we can do for him," Papa had said reasonably.

"At least we will be near him and can see him," Mother said. "He will know we are there."

Papa relented and told her to pack in a hurry.

In the meantime, all Bernie could do was try to be brave and wait. She sat silently beside Aunt Lolly as they drove to the farm. Dear Aunt Lolly, who was always there when someone needed her. She had even insisted that Sheppie come along with them. He did nothing these days but lie on the front porch, waiting for the boys to come home.

"Maybe he'll perk up a bit if he has a good run with the dogs at the farm," Aunt Lolly said.

Bernie felt that she and Sheppie were now two more of Aunt Lolly's strays to be taken in and cared for. She would share a bed in Lizzie's room. Lizzie had cleared out a dresser drawer for her to put her things.

Bernie knew that her cousins were doing their best to keep her spirits high. However, she could not help feeling a bit sad as she listened to their happy give-and-take around the Mifflin supper table. It was a stark contrast with the silence that had settled over her own family's table now that the boys were gone. She wondered if things would ever be the same again. She knew that she must not think about that right now.

Susie was telling the family about the paper she had written for school the previous year. "I had to report on a famous person. I chose Susan B. Anthony since I am named for her. She traveled around speaking out against slavery and getting women the vote. Sometimes people tried to stop her from speaking because she was a woman."

Her older sister, Peggy, not to be outdone, said, "I was named for Margaret Sanger, and she was famous, too. She tried to help women get the vote."

"We are all named for someone famous," Lizzie said, keeping the peace as always. "I was named for Elizabeth Cady Stanton. She worked to put an end to slavery and then helped start the women's suffrage movement."

Bernie looked directly at her cousin, Alice. "Now it's your turn to tell us who you were named for. Let's put an end to this mystery."

"What mystery?" Susie wanted to know.

"I want to know who Alice was named for," Bernie said. "Was it Alice Paul the famous suffragette?"

"Sorry, I wish I had been named for such an illustrious person," Alice said. "Sadly, I was born before Alice Paul came on the scene." That was all she said.

"Aunt Lolly, do tell us," Bernie begged.

Aunt Lolly laughed. "Well, it is a bit embarrassing. Embarrassing for me that is. You see I was very young when I married your Uncle Leroy. I was still reading books such as *Alice's Adventures in Wonderland*. I loved those stories, and I thought Alice was a pretty name."

Bernie said, "Is that all there is to it? That is a bit of a let-down."

"Why do you think I haven't told anyone?" Alice said. "I have three sisters who have been given the names of important women, but I was named for a fictional girl whose claim to fame was that she fell down a rabbit hole."

Bernie couldn't help but chuckle as Alice's little sisters burst into giggles.

That night, and every night for the next two weeks, Bernie went to sleep thanking God for the Mifflins and praying, "Please take care of Ben and Nick and Mother and Papa."

They were the longest two weeks of her life. She felt as though some of her prayers were answered when Mother and Papa sent a letter saying that Ben had passed the crisis. He was getting better. He was being discharged from the army. They would be bringing him home with them soon.

The evening she received that good news, she sat on the front porch of the Mifflin farm, petting Sheppie. "Now, all we have to worry about is Nick." Then she added, "And Jack."

17

An Unexpected Challenge

When Bernie walked up the hill to her home one warm July afternoon, she saw someone sitting in the porch swing with Mother. She was glad to see that it was Aunt Rose. The two women were drinking lemonade.

Bernie hurried across the grass, waving as she walked. She came up the three steps and perched herself on the railing. Mother went back inside to refill their glasses and get one for Bernie.

"What brings you here?" Bernie asked her aunt.

"I'm on a special mission."

"That sounds very mysterious."

"Not really. I'm recruiting volunteers."

"Does it have to do with Mother?"

"I had hoped your mother would want to join us. Perhaps she will decide she can do it at a later date."

"What kind of volunteers?"

"Several women from the Lafayette Franchise League have been going to the Indiana State Soldiers' Home. I thought you might like to go with me and help."

"What could I possibly do to be of help out there?" Bernie asked. "I don't know anything about nursing."

Aunt Rose laughed. "Neither do I, but there are lots of things for volunteers to do. It is mostly visiting with the soldiers. We help keep their spirits up. Their days stretch into a lot of lonely hours when they are away from family. Some of them get very discouraged at how slowly they are healing. It's mostly to show them that someone cares."

"I care, but what would I do? What would I say?"

"Sometimes you don't have to do or say a thing. Often it's a matter of listening. Or you could offer to read aloud or write a letter home for them."

Bernie thought about that for a moment, trying to imagine what it would be like. "Do they have injuries that are horrible to look at?"

Aunt Rose opened her mouth and then shut it again. She sighed and said, "Truthfully, there are some things that will break your heart to see or hear about."

"I don't know if I could do that," Bernie said.

"That's what your mother said. I understand, but don't say no until you have had a chance to think about it a while."

Later that afternoon as Bernie sat alone in her room, she thought about Ben who had nearly died from influenza. Mother and Papa had been by his bedside day and night, until they were able to bring him home. They were fortunate to be able to do that. But what about the soldier boys who didn't have parents nearby or who didn't have any family at all? Then, an even more horrible thought occurred to her—what if Nick was in a hospital somewhere and no one came to visit him?

Bernie got up from her desk and walked to the end of the long hallway and paused before the closed door of Nick's room. She turned the knob and let it swing open slowly. She inhaled sharply as she stood on the threshold and looked inside. It was just as she had seen it on the terrible day she found his note—unusually spick-and-span for happy-go-lucky Nick. She entered slowly, feeling a bit guilty at coming into his room when he was not there, but she had to be in touch with him somehow.

"Oh Nick, what shall I do?" she whispered to the silence. "Will it help if I go out to the hospital to visit with a veteran? I want to do it, but I am so scared. It might make me think of all the terrible things that could be happening to you." She suspected that was why Mother had refused Aunt Rose's request to go out to the Soldiers' Home.

Bernie went to Nick's desk and sat down in his chair. "Maybe if I had something of yours to carry with me, it would give me courage," she thought. Methodically she opened the drawers, one by one, hoping to find some way to be closer to him. What was she looking for? Perhaps some little memento that had meant something to him. The top drawer had pencils. The next drawer had paper. Nothing that she did not have in her own desk.

The large bottom drawer, however, held a large tin box. She remembered the long ago Christmas when it had been full of cookies from Aunt Lolly. It

People on the American home front helped with the war effort in many capacities. The American Red Cross worked at home and abroad during the war, providing healthcare to wounded and sick soldiers as well as providing recreation for veteran patients. Many adults and children volunteered for the American Red Cross. By the end of the war 20 million adults and 11 million children were members of the American Red Cross.

had a brightly colored picture of Santa's sleigh and reindeer on the top. "When it's empty can I have it?" she had asked. Immediately, each of the boys had said they wanted it, too. Papa had finally settled the argument by having them draw straws. Bernie remembered that she had stomped off angrily to her room when Nick won. "The boys always get everything they want," she had cried unreasonably as she climbed the stairs.

She had just crawled into her bed that evening when Nick knocked on her door and said, "You can have the box."

"No," she said. "I don't want it now." She remembered that she had not even bothered to say thank you for his generous offer.

Now Bernie pulled the box out of the drawer and removed the lid. It was his treasure box. Inside she found a tangled collection of string, a leather pouch containing his pocket knife, a pack of baseball cards, and two arrowheads. She recoiled when she also discovered the shriveled carcass of a dead frog. Carefully she laid each item out on the desktop in front of her. On the very bottom she saw an envelope. She hesitated before opening it. It might be something private for his eyes only. She noticed that the flap was not sealed, so she convinced herself that it couldn't be that private. Gingerly she looked inside. There was a newspaper clipping. It was carefully folded, although it gave evidence of having been crumpled up at one time. She unfolded it and smoothed it out. The headline read: "WINNING ESSAY. A Fourteen-year-old Girl Wins Contest with Her Essay, 'Who Speaks for the Women?'"

Bernie shook her head in disbelief. It was her essay—her Lafayette Franchise League essay! Nick had saved it in his treasure box. He had not told her at the time, but he must have been proud of her to have kept it.

She had come up to his room for an answer about whether or not she should go to the Soldiers' Home. She had needed something to give her courage and now she knew what she must do.

She sat with tears running down her cheeks as she put everything back the way it had been. As Bernie stood and turned to leave the room, she saw Ben standing in the doorway.

"How long have you been there?" Bernie asked.

"Long enough," he said as he held out his arms. She walked toward him. He folded his arms around her and wiped away her tears and his own with his sleeve.

"I miss him, too," Ben said.

A few minutes later, Bernie went downstairs to the telephone and asked the operator to connect her to Aunt Rose. "Please let me know what day you are going out to the veterans' hospital. I will go with you," Bernie promised.

That evening at the supper table, she waited for an opportune time to get her parents' permission. She asked just as Papa was taking a large bite of Mother's homemade cherry pie. He almost choked on it. Mother dashed into the kitchen to get a drink of water for him.

"What in the world will you think of doing next?" Papa sputtered.

"As a matter of fact," Bernie said calmly. "It was Aunt Rose's idea. She goes out there once a week. She asked me to come with her."

He pursed his lips tightly. She was afraid he was going to say, "No."

"I'm doing it because of Nick," Bernie said.

Mother came back into the dining room. As she handed Papa a glass of water, she put her hand on Papa's arm and looked at him without saying a word. Papa didn't speak either. He just nodded. Bernie got up from the table and put her arms around him and hugged him.

The following Saturday afternoon, Bernie tried to decide which dress she should wear. Finally, she selected a plain navy blue shirtwaist. She wondered if she should wear a hat and gloves, as though this were a proper social call, such as the ones she and Mother made when they went to see Grandmother Epperson. She finally decided to wear a small white straw boater. She pulled a scarf from the drawer to tie her hat on her head as they rode in Grandmother Epperson's open touring car. She could carry gloves in case she needed them.

Bernie looked through her desk to find writing paper and a pen. She wanted to be prepared if she was asked to write a letter. She started down the stairs and then turned back. Perhaps she ought to take a book, too. She looked at the books on her shelf. What would be appropriate for a wounded soldier? She doubted that anything she had would be appropriate. What soldier would want to hear her read books that were meant for young girls? Bernie considered Helen Keller's autobiography. That might be good inspiration as it was about someone overcoming seemingly insurmountable challenges. Then she thought that perhaps her brothers would have something more appropriate. She went to Nick's room, but found mostly books about war. There was the *Personal Memoirs of U.S. Grant* as well as *Lew Wallace, an Autobiography*. She shook her head thinking that a war story might not be such a good idea, either.

Once again Bernie was overwhelmed with doubts about what would happen today. Why in the world had she promised Aunt Rose she would do this? She almost wished Papa had forbidden her to go. Her hands were shaking and her knees felt weak. Perhaps it wasn't too late to change her mind.

Bernie was about to tell her aunt that she simply could not do this when she noticed a dog-eared copy of Mark Twain's *The Adventures of Tom Sawyer*. That had been one of Nick's favorite books. In fact, she sometimes thought that Nick was a lot like Tom Sawyer. The book was covered with dust, and she looked for a cloth to wipe it off. She smiled sadly as she realized how much she missed him. She reminded herself that she was doing this for Nick, and maybe even for Jack, too. But, in a way, she also had to do this for herself. She could not join the army as her brothers had, but she could try to be brave today.

"It's a lovely day for a drive," Mother called pleasantly as Bernie climbed up into the seat of the auto. She was surprised to see Aunt Rose in the driver's

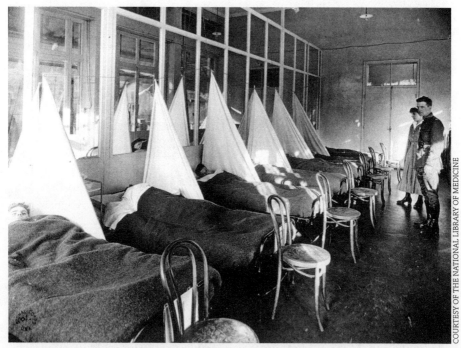

COURTESY OF THE NATIONAL LIBRARY OF MEDICINE

World War I was unlike any war before it due to the introduction of new weapons, such as machine guns, and chemical weapons, such as mustard gas. Poisonous gas caused blistering and burning, and it also suffocated and blinded soldiers. From May 1918 to June 1919 nearly 10,000 patients passed through the doors of this hospital, U.S. Army Camp Hospital Number 45, located in Aix-les-Bain, France. On top of all the war casualties, camp hospitals such as this were also overwhelmed by the numbers of men struck down by influenza. Pictured here is an influenza ward separated from the other wards by glass.

seat. Usually Grandmother Epperson's handy man, Thomas, drove whenever she or Aunt Rose went somewhere.

"When did you learn to drive?" Bernie asked as she climbed up and settled herself on the warm leather seat.

"I started learning this past spring. I'd kept thinking about your essay that was published in the newspaper last year," Aunt Rose said. "You see, what you wrote was good for me. I decided to become more independent. So, I asked your Aunt Lolly to teach me."

"I think it's wonderful," Bernie said. "But, what does Grandmother think about it?"

Aunt Rose turned and looked sternly at Bernie over the top of her round spectacles.

"Perhaps we ought to let this be our little secret," Aunt Rose said. "I only take the machine out when your grandmother is having her nap."

Bernie didn't know whether to laugh or cheer.

They crossed the bridge and drove parallel to the river on the west side. It was, as Mother had said, a wonderful day for a drive. If only it were just a pleasure drive. Bernie took a deep breath and expelled it loudly.

"You will be all right," Aunt Rose said. "I was terribly nervous the first time I came out to the hospital. Just pretend you are talking with a friend or a relative. I brought some homemade sugar cookies and that usually is an ice-breaker. Remind me to give you some to share."

Aunt Rose stopped at the front desk to ask about her soldier and introduce Bernie.

The woman at the desk smiled a crinkly smile. "Oh, good. I think our boys always like to talk to a pretty girl." Then, realizing what she had said might cause hurt feelings, quickly added, "Not that they aren't glad to see you, Rose. I know the young man you visit always looks forward to having you come."

Aunt Rose smiled and nodded her head.

"Now, tell me," the nurse asked Bernie, "Do you both want to visit Rose's friend or would you like to see one of the soldiers by yourself?"

Bernie didn't have time to say, "Oh, I would prefer to go with my aunt."

Instead, Aunt Rose spoke up and said, "I am sure there are many boys who would like a visitor. I think she will do just fine on her own."

A nurse led Bernie down a long, dimly lit hall that was painted a dreadful pea-green color. It smelled of disinfectant that clashed with the aroma of thick paste wax on the wooden floors. They passed uniformed attendants pushing men in wheelchairs. Some of the patients had bandaged arms or legs. One man slumped limply to one side and his hands were curled up into gnarled fists. It was all that Bernie could do to keep from running in the other direction. She was gulping in air and exhaling it frantically. What if she fainted? That would be so embarrassing. As they reached the door of a ward with rows of beds on either side, the nurse paused and turned to her.

"These boys have experienced things that none of us will ever know first-hand. Many of them have no idea what the future holds for them. They need your friendship. Introduce yourself and talk about anything that comes into your mind."

"I'll try," Bernie hardly recognized the sound of her own choked-up voice.

She followed the nurse into the room. A man sat in a wheelchair near the window. His head was swathed in bandages.

"Someone is here to visit you, Vincent," the nurse said.

The man did not turn his head to look at Bernie as she approached. The nurse pulled a wooden chair up next to him.

"I'll be back to get you in an hour," the nurse said and left them.

Bernie's stomach flip-flopped. An hour! What in the world would she do for an entire hour?

Bernie sat down and realized that not only was the man's head bandaged, his eyes were bandaged, too. There were holes in the bandage, cut for his nose and mouth, but he did not speak.

After a long awkward silence, Bernie managed to say faintly, "Hello, my name is Bernice Epperson, but everybody calls me Bernie."

There was no reply.

"I've lived here all my life. I go to the high school in town across the river. I'll be sixteen soon."

Even though there was no response from the man in the wheelchair, Bernie continued to talk. "My papa owns a store on the courthouse square. It's called Epperson's Emporium. I have two brothers. Both of my brothers joined the army. My oldest brother, Ben, almost died from influenza, so they sent him back home. Now he works in my father's store. Papa wants him to take over the business someday, but Ben does not want to do this. He wants to be a photographer and explore the West. My father says that is a silly idea. He says no one can earn a living by being a photographer. My other brother, Nick, ran away to join the army when he was sixteen, and we don't know where he is.

We all miss him very much, even our dog, Sheppie. Sheppie lies on the porch all day in front of the door, just waiting for him to come back."

Bernie started to cry and could not stop. She got up and ran from the room. She stood outside in the hallway and leaned against the awful green wall to sob. This turned into hiccups that shook her body.

A nurse came and brought her a glass of water. The nurse put a comforting arm around Bernie's shoulder. "You'll be all right."

The nurse went inside the room and came back out shortly. "As soon as you catch your breath, Vincent would like for you to come back and talk to him some more."

"I can't," Bernie's voice was trembling. "I can't do this. I've made such a mess of things. I just babbled on and on like an idiot. Whatever must he think of me?"

"He told me that he wishes he had a sister like you."

18

Discord

Later that summer, sixteen-year-old Bernie and her Aunt Rose arrived only a few minutes before a Lafayette Franchise League meeting began. To their surprise the room was packed. There was a low, disconcerting murmur throughout the hall. Bernie had an uneasy premonition that something ominous was about to happen.

Alice hurried up to them. "We tried to save seats for you with us but no luck. We did manage to find two seats together for you several rows behind us. See, Lizzie is holding them for you."

Bernie turned and saw Lizzie wave from seats about halfway back.

"What's going on?" Bernie asked.

"I'm not certain, but I think trouble is brewing," Alice said, as she and Lizzie hurried back to their seats next to Aunt Lolly in the second row and the sound of the president's gavel called the meeting to order.

Bernie knew that many of the suffragists were determined to continue the struggle to get a constitutional amendment passed so that women would have the right to vote in all elections. Others were convinced that this had to take a back seat to the war effort. The issue had caused disagreements in the last several meetings, but tonight she detected disturbing signs that they had reached a breaking point.

After the meeting had been called to order and the opening ceremonies conducted, the president called for reports. Bernie sighed deeply. So far, everything seemed to be progressing as usual. Maybe it would be okay.

The woman who headed up the Knitting Project spoke first. "I am proud to report that we have made and sent a total of two hundred and six pairs of woolen socks to our soldiers overseas." There was a smattering of polite applause. "In addition, we are knitting scarves and hope to increase. . . ." The woman trailed off as an undercurrent of voices began buzzing like angry bees throughout the crowd. The president pounded her gavel once more and called for order. The woman's voice was a bit shaky as she continued her report, "For those of you who do not knit, we ask that you donate. . . ."

"That's all very well and good," a member interrupted from the rear. "I concede that these are useful things to do. However, we have been meeting together here for a very long time, united for the one important purpose of getting the vote for women." Bernie and Aunt Rose turned to look back and see who had spoken. It was a tall, thin woman with a surprisingly strong voice. "When are we going to get down to the business we really came here to do?"

A few women backed her up, saying, "Yes. Yes. That's right."

Another woman joined in, "We need to remember that we are the Lafayette Franchise League, part of the National American Woman Suffrage Association. We are not the Red Cross, as important as their work may be."

There were cries of approval for this speaker from all sides.

A strident voice called out in opposition, "We must put the suffrage cause aside until after the war is over."

The president rapped and called for order again, but the members continued arguing.

"This is no time to lose sight of our purpose," said the tall, thin woman who had first spoken up. "We have come so far, made so much progress, we dare not quit. If we stop now, we won't stay where we are, we will go backward. We'll have to build up steam all over again."

Another woman rose and shouted indignantly, "Our country is at war. Our boys—our sons—are going overseas to fight. We must support them. How will it look if we continue to press for our own selfish interests and ignore our troops?"

Before she had taken her seat, another woman jumped up and added, "I say it is downright unpatriotic for us to put our desire for the vote ahead of their well-being."

"No, it is more unpatriotic for us to give up on such a noble cause."

Bernie saw an older white-haired woman in the front row stand up. She recognized this woman who lived in one of the big houses up on the hill not far from where Grandmother Epperson lived. The woman's voice was soft at first, but grew stronger as she spoke, "Those of you who know me, know that I've been working for women's suffrage for a good many years. I don't have much time to wait. I want to see women get the vote before I die."

AS A WAR MEASURE

The Country is Asking of Women Service	Women Are Asking of The Country
AS	
FARMERS	
MECHANICS	
NURSES and DOCTORS	
MUNITION WORKERS	
MINE WORKERS	
YEOMEN	
GAS MAKERS	
BELL BOYS	
MESSENGERS	ENFRANCHISEMENT
CONDUCTORS	
MOTORMEN	
ARMY COOKS	
TELEGRAPHERS	
AMBULANCE DRIVERS	
ADVISORS TO THE COUNCIL OF NATIONAL DEFENSE	
AND	
The Country is Getting It !	**Are the Women Going to Get It ?**

National Woman Suffrage Publishing Company, Inc. 144   171 Madison Ave., New York City

During World War I women were asked to take over jobs left by men going to war. They worked on farms, in factories, and in other service industries. It was also the first time women were allowed to serve in the Navy and Marine Corps, filling positions such as nurses and as yeomen, serving as clerks. This National Woman Suffrage poster illustrates that women filled many roles during the war but only asked for one thing in return—the vote.

Loud applause erupted after the woman sat down.

Then Bernie heard the voice of her former third grade teacher. "President Wilson says we are fighting this war to make the world safe for democracy. What kind of a democracy is it that won't allow women to vote?"

Calls of "Amen" echoed throughout the hall.

The members' voices grew louder—with more emotion and vehemence. The women ignored another call for order from their president.

"We were so close to achieving what we want with the Maston–McKinley Bill. I say press on."

"But Indiana's supreme court ruled it unconstitutional."

"Is that a reason for us to abandon our cause and all our sisters in states that have not moved forward at all?"

"The only way to secure our rights is to work for a federal constitutional amendment."

"Well, I have a son in the army and I'm going to continue to knit socks and write letters and do everything I can to support him and the other soldiers. The vote can wait."

LIBRARY OF CONGRESS, MANUSCRIPT DIVISION, "MRS. SUSANNA MORIN SWING," RECORDS OF THE NATIONAL WOMAN'S PARTY

While many women supported the war effort, there were also many women involved in the suffrage movement who felt war work was taking away from fighting for the right to vote. One of the arguments, as seen in this photograph of Susanna Morin Swing, was that rather than fighting to keep democracy safe around the world, democracy should begin at home.

"Don't forget, though, there are women serving our country overseas as nurses. And, even they cannot vote. What are we doing for them?"

The voices for and against working for suffrage bounced back and forth so quickly, becoming louder and louder, that it was almost impossible for anyone to be heard. The president again pounded her gavel on the podium, but no one seemed to pay any attention.

A booming voice called out, "I know not what course you in this hall are going to take, but as for me, I want to be part of a group that stands behind our country in its struggle."

One determined woman stood and answered, "Very well. If that is the way you want it, you just put on the brakes. There are a lot of us who are going to continue to work so we can vote. Perhaps if women had the vote we wouldn't be fighting this war. We've marched together for this cause before. I ask all of you who are determined to get the vote for women to follow me." Next, the most disturbing sounds of all reached Bernie's ears—chairs being pushed aside and people standing and then marching from the room. She was horrified to see almost half of their group leaving. Many of these were women who had become her friends during the trip to Washington, DC. They were dedicated women, and she wanted to march with them again.

Bernie did not know what to do. The arguments of both sides were so convincing. But then she thought of Nick and Ben. She felt that if she marched out now, she would somehow betray her own brothers. She thought about Jack—kind, thoughtful Jack who had always stuck up for her. No matter how terrible she had been to him, he had always been there for her. She thought of her new friend Vincent, out at the veterans' hospital. She could not give up her weekly visits to him. She had to do everything in her power to help the war effort even though her heart was with the suffragists who wanted the vote.

Bernie's heart did a sickening flip-flop inside her chest. She saw Aunt Lolly, Alice, and Lizzie moving out into the aisles to join the others who were leaving. Aunt Lolly's eyes were red and her cheeks glistened with tears. Lizzie ducked her head as she passed the row where Bernie and Aunt Rose sat. Only Alice turned their way with a questioning look on her face, but Bernie could not decipher what her cousin meant by the expression.

Bernie turned toward Aunt Rose and asked, "What do we do now?"

Aunt Rose shook her head in dismay.

"Tell me. What should I do?" Bernie pleaded. "Why does it have to be so hard?"

"I can't make this decision for you, Bernie."

Bernie started to stand, but Aunt Rose stayed seated. Bernie sat down again. At least she would have Aunt Rose on her side. She would not be completely alone with her choice.

When the dissenters had gone, the meeting continued. Everyone who remained in the room seemed subdued. Bernie could barely force herself to listen to the rest of the reports. How could this have happened? What would this do to her family? Could they ever have good times together after this split? She remembered the stories she had heard of families who had been deeply divided and torn apart over the issue of slavery during the Civil War. Bernie didn't think she could stand it if anything like that happened to her family because of a difference of opinion. What would it be like at school if Lizzie never spoke to her again? What if Alice never came over to take her out in the car again? What if there were no more family gatherings at the farm? She wondered if she had made the correct decision.

Bernie learned the answer to her troubling questions after the meeting was over. When she and Aunt Rose went out into the fresh evening air, they saw many of the league members who had walked out. Several were still standing in small groups talking. Bernie saw Aunt Lolly, Alice, and Lizzie. She took a deep breath, not knowing what to do or say.

She looked over at Lizzie, and Lizzie stared back. Lizzie seemed as puzzled as she was. Bernie saw Aunt Lolly look up and glance in her direction. Aunt Lolly grabbed Lizzie's hand and deliberately walked toward Bernie. Alice followed along.

"It's all right," Aunt Lolly said softly. "You made your choice. We made ours, but that isn't going to change anything between us. We will always love each other."

Bernie felt Aunt Lolly's arm around her shoulder, and Lizzie reached out to take her hand. "It's all right for loved ones not to agree," Aunt Lolly said.

They smiled half-heartedly at this, but they knew this was not going to be easy for them. They stood for a few moments in awkward silence, not knowing what else to say.

Bernie walked quietly with Aunt Rose to her car. Neither Bernie nor Aunt Rose spoke on the ride home. Each was deep in her own thoughts. Bernie felt wounded, but this was a wounding of a different kind than she had ever known.

When Bernie entered the house she saw Papa dozing in his chair in the front parlor. She looked at him and thought how much older he looked these days. Even though he kept his worries to himself so as not to upset Mother, recent events were taking a terrible toll on him. She wanted to put her arms around him and let him know she cared, but she did not want to disturb him. Instead, Bernie tiptoed up the stairs to her room. She didn't want to have to talk about the disagreements of this evening. She was certain that it would seem of little consequence to him compared to the worry about Nick.

Perhaps Aunt Rose would take her out to the Soldiers' Home tomorrow to see Vincent. He had become someone she could talk to easily. It was strange that considering the problems he was facing, he always had time to listen to others. She remembered how she had been so nervous about that first visit to the Home when she met him. Now, she felt that she could tell him anything.

19

OCTOBER 1918
Mad Dog

It had been an unusually warm day for early October. After her last class at school, Bernie rode the streetcar as far as Courthouse Square. She stopped in at Epperson's Emporium to say hello to Ben and Papa. She hoped that Ben would offer to take her to Graeber's Soda Fountain for something cool to drink. But Ben wasn't there.

"He isn't here." Papa pursed his lips as he added, "He said he was going to hear a guest speaker at the Camera Club. Some fellow from that *National Geographic* magazine."

Bernie knew that Papa was annoyed Ben wasn't there to help him with the office work. Ben had long since graduated from stocking the shelves to tallying up the receipts at the end of the day. She also suspected that Papa was even more upset since the lecturer was speaking on a subject that would encourage Ben's wanderlust.

Just as Bernie was leaving the store, Papa called to her. "Oh, I almost forgot. Mother wants you to stop at the grocery and buy a couple pounds of flour."

Bernie decided to have a soda by herself before she went to the grocery. She ordered her favorite cherry phosphate and carried it to one of the small tables. She opened her notebook to finish a letter she had begun to a soldier and reread the words she had already written:

Dear Doughboy,

That is an odd name to call our soldiers. I hope you don't mind if I call you that, but since I do not know your name, I thought it might be all right. I read that the name "Doughboy" came about because our soldiers used to mix up bread dough and bake it in their helmets. My cousin Alice says she does not believe it. What do you think? I have two older brothers. One is named Ben. He was in the army for a while, but he had influenza and almost died, so he was discharged and is back home again. My other brother, Nick, is too young to be a soldier, but he ran off and joined anyway. We do not know where he is. My mother is sick with worry about him. We keep hoping that he will write and tell us that he is okay. But we haven't heard a thing.

She could not finish the horrible thought that was always lodged in a dark corner of her mind. Bernie looked at what she had written and shook her head in disgust. What a stupid, boring letter it was! She had volunteered to write to soldiers, and she was doing the best she could. However, she could not imagine that anyone would want to read this one no matter how desperate he was to receive mail. She stuffed it, unfinished, back inside her notebook. She would finish it later. Maybe she'd think of something more interesting to say tonight. She sucked the last cold drop of her drink through the straw and left Graeber's.

Bernie plodded up the Union Street hill as she headed home. Her arms were full. It had been chilly this morning, so she had worn her coat, but now it was too hot to wear. She also carried her schoolbooks and the bag of flour Mother had wanted her to buy. She felt dismal about everything in general.

Today had not been one of her better days at school. Bernie thought she had studied hard enough for her math test, but she had drawn a complete blank on the final question. Worse yet, Lizzie had gotten every answer correct. It was not that she wished her cousin bad luck, it was just that the two of them had been competing ever since they started school. Lizzie was determined to be class valedictorian, as Alice had been. Bernie had made up her mind that she was going to win that honor.

Every step she took in the Indian summer sunshine made her feel grumpier than ever. Bernie was sunk in her own misery until she noticed a limping soldier in a well-worn uniform, slowly making his way up the hill ahead of her. He appeared to be even more weary than she felt. His shoulders slumped and he leaned heavily on a cane. He carried a cumbersome duffle bag in his other hand. She could tell that every step he took was an effort for him. As Bernie watched him she felt ashamed of feeling so sorry for herself. She wondered how far he had come and where he was going.

Many children wrote letters to soldiers, as Bernie does in this chapter, as part of the home front war effort. This is a letter from Beatrice Williams, an African American student in Indianapolis, to her former teacher, Irven Armstrong, who was a sergeant in the 351st Field Artillery in France. The letter states:

> 934 Fayette St.
> Indianapolis, Ind.
> Nov. 7, 1918

Sergeant Armstrong,

I am a pupil of No. 17 School. My name is Beatrice Williams. You were at one time my Mathematics teacher. The letter you wrote to the pupils of this school was received. I enjoyed listening to it being read to us by Miss Walker. All of the school children are doing all they can to help the men and boys who have gone Over There. We still have our Air Plane races and each child does all he can to see that his room gets in the lead. We are bringing peach seeds to school to be used in making carbon for gas masks. A Liberty Loan drive began here Oct. 28th and from the way the papers read the colored people did their bit. We children are buying Thrift Stamps and War Stamps. The teachers still give us our buttons to show where we rank in the Thrift Army. I am corporal now but by the time this letter reaches you I hope to be Sergt.

There has been an epidemic of Influenza here and the schools, churches and all places of amus[e]ment were closed for four weeks. During the last week fewer cases were reported so everything opened again and we are back in school. I was a victim of the Influenza but I am alright now.

> Yours sincerely,
> Beatrice Williams

Bernie was glad to be nearing home. She longed to sit in the swing on the front porch, cooled by the shade of the tall maples in the yard.

When the man ahead of her was opposite the Epperson house, he paused and put down his bag. He reached into his back pocket and pulled out a large handkerchief and wiped his forehead. He stood, looking in the direction of the house. She thought he might appreciate a drink of cold water. Bernie walked a bit faster, wondering what Mother would say if she invited the man to come up on their porch to rest for a while before he went on his way.

She was surprised when she saw him take a few steps up into the front yard. At that moment, she heard Sheppie's frenzied barking. The old dog came bounding across the grass toward the man. Bernie hadn't seen their dog move with that much energy in years. She saw Sheppie leap up on the man.

Bernie was horrified. "Here, Sheppie. Come here. Stop that!" The dog paid no attention to her. Bernie continued to shout at the dog, "Sheppie, what do you think you're doing? Let him alone."

Bernie was certain Sheppie had gone mad in this miserable heat. What else would make him attack someone that way? Maybe there was something about the stranger that seemed threatening to the dog. Did Sheppie think he was protecting his family when the man stepped on the grass?

Bernie dropped everything she was carrying and ran in that direction, still calling to the dog. Sheppie ignored her commands and repeatedly jumped at the man, almost knocking him off his feet. Bernie saw the man kneel slowly, put his arms around the dog and bury his head in the dog's shaggy fur.

"Oh, I am so sorry." Bernie hurried forward to apologize. "I've never seen him attack anyone before."

Bernie stopped short. She realized that Sheppie was not attacking the stranger. He was licking the man's face. Then she saw the face clearly. Bernie started to scream at the top of her lungs, "Nick! Nick! Is it really you?" Bernie grabbed his shoulders and put her arms around his neck. The two of them toppled onto the lawn as the dog ran in circles around them, yelping with excitement.

"Oh, Nick. We never thought we'd see you again. We thought you were. . . . " She pressed her fingers over her mouth, horrified at what she had almost said. Instead she asked, "Are you okay? Does anyone else know that you've come home?"

He shook his head. "I'm so tired," he said. "Let me rest awhile." He lay back on the grass. Sheppie flopped down next to him, still licking his face.

Bernie heard the familiar rasping sound of the screen hinge as the front door opened. She saw her mother step onto the porch. Mother's hand went up to her eyes to shield them from the late afternoon sun. "What's all the commotion out here?"

"Oh, Mother," Bernie cried. "Mother. Come and see. Nick is home."

For a moment, Mother seemed frozen to the spot. Her knees sagged and seemed about to give way. She reached out for the porch railing to steady herself. Then she shrieked and ran down the steps, onto the lawn, and toward the place where Nick and Sheppie lay on the grass.

This wall telephone is similar to the one Bernie would have had in her home in 1918.

Bernie stared as the misery of the last year was erased from her mother's face. She thought Mother seemed to grow younger with each step she took. As Mother ran, hairpins flew from her hair. A long strand fell loose. It bounced up and down like a spring, coiling and uncoiling. At the sight of it, Bernie started to laugh hysterically.

Mother threw herself down across Nick's chest. "Oh, my boy. My dear, dear boy. You've come back to us. Thank God."

Sheppie sprang into action once more, invigorated by the excitement. He ran around and around the spot where the three of them lay. He paused first by Nick, next by Bernie, and finally by Mother. He seemed unable to make up his mind whose face he should lick first, so he licked them all. Bernie laughed, remembering that Mother had never been that fond of the smelly creature, yet now she giggled like a schoolgirl and repeated, "I'm so happy. I am so happy. My boy is home."

Bernie managed to get to her feet. She ran into the house to ring Papa at the store. Once more, Sheppie felt obliged to be part of the action, darting in front of her and making her stumble over him.

She cranked the handle on the telephone to get the operator so she could ask her to dial the Emporium. It seemed forever until Papa's voice came on the line.

Bernie shouted, "Nick is home. Nick is home. Come and see him, Papa."

Bernie did not wait to hear his answer if there was any. She dashed back outside to where Mother now sat on the grass with Nick resting his head in her lap.

By this time, several neighbors had arrived to join the celebration. Bernie knew that the operator had listened in on her telephone call and was now busy informing everyone in town. For once, Bernie was glad to have a busybody telephone operator.

There was quite a welcome delegation assembled in front of the Epperson house by the time the Hupmobile came chugging up the hill. Ben was at the wheel, honking the horn. Papa leaned forward, ready to spring out before the car stopped by the curb. For once, neither Papa nor Mother seemed to care what the neighbors thought about the Epperson family and their behavior. Nick was back home again, and that was all that mattered to them right now.

Bernie was engulfed in a kaleidoscope of sounds and sights and emotions. The telephone was ringing inside the house. Outside there was laughter and

When soldiers came home, it was a big deal for family and friends. In this photograph from May 1919, Frank C. Henry is surrounded by family and friends after he marched in a Welcome Home Day parade in Indianapolis that ended in Military Park.

weeping. Everyone was talking at once. Questions and more questions hovered unanswered in the air. Bernie's head felt light, and she thought her chest was going to burst with the how and why of it all. It occurred to her that this must be how a miracle feels.

Bernie saw Papa helping Mother to her feet. She still held Nick's hand in hers and he managed to get to his feet. Somehow through the clamor, Bernie heard Nick say softly, "I would like to go inside now." However, groups of neighbors surrounded him, and he was engulfed with handshakes, hugs, and well wishes for the moment.

20

The Letter

It wasn't a dream. Nick was back, but in a most unsettling, inexplicable way, he was not really back. At least, he was not the Nick who had left their home more than a year ago. There was no trace of the teasing, wisecracking person he had been. His body was bulkier but not fat. He had put on muscle. He was a man—no longer a boy. But he was a man that Bernie had trouble recognizing as her brother.

Bernie watched him and sensed that it was an effort for him to respond to the many greetings of friends and neighbors who came, wanting to be part of the happy occasion. Even though Nick turned in their direction, his eyes seemed to be looking inward at sights he did not want to see—sights he could not blot out by blinking them away. When friends welcomed him home, he shook hands and responded with a polite, if subdued, "Thank you." But there was a distance that no one, not even family, seemed to be able to bridge. His face was etched with pain.

After the family had finally gone inside the house, Nick looked around as though he was trying to convince himself that he belonged there. He often leaned over to pet Sheppie—the dog seeming to be his anchor in a sea of unreality. He moved about the house touching the furniture, turning lamps on and off. He hunched over as though he carried a burden. It was a terrible burden, the family learned.

"Sit down," Mother urged. "Or would you rather lie down? Are you in pain? Is your leg hurting?"

"I'm okay," Nick assured her.

He put his hand inside his jacket pocket and pulled out a crumpled, dirty envelope. He put it in Bernie's hand. "We all wrote letters before we. . . ." He did not finish his sentence. "I promised Jack I would give this to you if I made it home."

Bernie looked at it, puzzled. Why would Jack write a letter to her? Bernie stood looking at it, wondering when she should open it.

Nick said, "Jack is not coming home." He took a deep, unsteady breath. "I've got to go over and tell Mr. McClarty."

"Wait until you've rested a bit and had your supper," Mother said.

"No, I must to do this right away," Nick insisted. "I have to tell him as soon as possible that Jack is buried in a grave in France. I can't rest or do anything until I have done that."

Nick's voice broke and great sobs wracked his body. Papa stepped nearer and put his arms around his son. The two of them stood holding onto each other. Bernie could not bear to watch them and turned away. Ben put his arm around her shoulder and reached out to enfold Mother, too. Bernie thought her heart was going to explode inside her chest.

It was a long time before Papa said, "It's too far for you to walk to McClarty's. We'll take you there."

Bernie watched them leave. Ben was driving. Nick rode in back with Papa.

Bernie and Mother stayed home. While they waited for the men to return, they went into the kitchen. Mother was intent on cooking all of Nick's favorite foods. She called Edna to ask if she could bring one of her chickens to fry. Next, she decided to add a ham to the menu. Mother had just put it in the oven when she said, "Macaroni and cheese. He loves macaroni and cheese. Should I bake a pie or a cake? Maybe I should make both."

Together Mother and Bernie cooked enough food for an army. They cooked because they needed to keep busy while they waited. They cooked because Nick was back safely under their roof where they could see and touch him. They cooked because they wanted to see him in his usual place at the dinner table. They cooked to convince themselves that Nick being home was not a dream.

At supper time, Nick made a brave attempt to sit at the table and eat as though it were old times. Before long, however, he apologized to Mother and excused himself from the table after eating only a few bites.

"Would you mind very much if I went up to bed now?" he asked.

Ben picked up Nick's heavy duffel bag, but Nick insisted that he could do it for himself.

The family watched helplessly as he went upstairs, leaning heavily on the banister, his face pale and his knees shaking. Sheppie mirrored his demeanor. The dog's nails clicked rhythmically on the wooden floor as he plodded up the steps following his beloved Nick.

Mother rose from her place as though she meant to go upstairs, too, but Papa reached out and put his hand on her arm, "Let him go. He needs to be by himself for a while. It has been a very difficult day for him."

After they heard Nick's door close, they all sat silently and stared at their plates, heaped with food left untouched. It was then that Papa and Ben told Bernie and Mother what had happened when they went to the McClarty place.

Nick had insisted that Papa and Ben wait outside for him in the automobile. He told them this was something he had to do on his own.

Nick was only inside McClarty's blacksmith shop a short time. When he came outside again he was leaning heavily on his cane, his limp seeming more pronounced than before. He was followed by McClarty, who waved a pair of tongs at him. McClarty's face was as red as his glowing tongs as he shouted,

More than 4.7 million Americans served during the First World War. Of these, more than 200,000 were wounded, and more than 100,000 were either killed, missing in action, or prisoners of war. Like Jack and Nick, many who fought on the front lines were barely out of boyhood.

"Now, I don't have any son left to help me. You and your foolish war talk. I remember how you always was. From the time you was a little boy, you said you was going to be a soldier. Well, you got your war. You took my boy. You took my only son along with you to play your stupid games. I wish he never met you. Then he would still be here to help me. Who will help me when I get too old to work?"

Mother buried her face in her napkin and her body shook silently with a grief too deep for sound or tears. Papa stood behind her chair and put a hand on each of her shoulders and leaned forward to whisper in her ear. Bernie looked away. She had never seen her parents like this.

Ben threw his napkin on his chair and went out on the front porch. Bernie followed her brother. It wasn't fair. Nick was home. They should not be so miserable. They should be having a party. Ben sat on the wooden railing and Bernie leaned against a post. She turned her face upward into the cool evening breeze, hoping it would soothe the pain. They were all together now as a

It was not uncommon for soldiers to write "just in case" letters to family and friends that would only be delivered in the event of the soldier's death, much like Jack's letter to Bernie. The soldiers here are from the American Expeditionary Forces, Company B, 316th Military Police, 91st Division. The picture was taken on August 31, 1918, in Montigny de Roi, Haute Marne, France.

family. This should be the happiest time in their lives, but she wondered if they would ever be truly happy again.

That evening when she went to her room to do her homework, she picked up the envelope from Jack. She looked at the dirt smudges—dirt from France. He had written this on a faraway battlefield, perhaps the place where the young man from Indiana had died.

Bernie opened the envelope. There was only one page. She smoothed the wrinkled sheet. It was not easy to read the words Jack had written. She seemed to be looking at them through crystal globes of tears that would not stop flowing.

My dear, dear Bernie,

Now I can write to you the words that I was never brave enough to say aloud, even though I wanted to. It is not courage that makes me write them now, because I know that if you are reading this, I will not be coming home to see the look on your face. Don't feel too bad. I really did not plan to come home after the war anyway. There was no life for me there. I did not want to work in my father's blacksmith shop. That was why I ran away to join the army. Nick always said he wanted to be a soldier, so it wasn't too hard for me to talk him into coming with me. I hope your family, and especially you, can forgive me for doing that.

I love you, Bernie. I always loved you and I always will. I know that you could never feel about me as I feel about you. Try not to be sad about this or about anything. I just hope you have a happy life and maybe think of me once in a while.

Yours, Jack

Bernie reread Jack's letter several times. Had it really said what she thought it did? If what Jack wrote was true, it had not been Nick who had talked Jack into joining the army. Her brother wasn't to blame for them running away. But why didn't Nick say so? Why hadn't Nick told this to Mr. McClarty?

Bernie clutched Jack's letter in her hand as she threw herself on her bed. She buried her face in her pillow so that she could scream with anger at the unfairness of it all. How could Jack's father have acted that way? That awful man seemed to feel worse that he had lost a lackey to help him in his blacksmith shop than he did about the fact that his son had been killed.

When her rage had worn her out, she lay quietly thinking about Jack. Jack was never coming back—Jack, who had always stood up for her and defended her. The memories from those long-ago times tumbled over themselves in her mind. She remembered how he had shared his food with her the day she had followed the boys out to the barn where they were building the plane. She remembered how he had followed her when she walked around the pond because he knew she was afraid of the dark. She remembered the day out at the old fort when they all looked for treasures, and she hadn't found one until she looked in her bait bucket and saw the cobalt blue bead.

She got up and went over to her desk. She opened one of the drawers and rummaged through it, until she came up with a small box. Inside was the bead still strung on a loop of fishing line. She slipped it over her head. It hung close to her heart.

"I'm so sorry, Jack. I wasn't always as nice to you as I should have been. I hope you will forgive me." She stood staring out at the darkness beyond her window. She knew that Jack had been right when he said that she would never be able to feel about him as he felt about her. She was ashamed because she had failed to appreciate how gentle and kind he was. Alice had been right about that. Bernie knew that Alice had been right about something else— Bernie's attitude toward Jack was snobbish. She wrapped her fingers around the bead and whispered, "You were too good for me, Jack."

She needed to talk to someone who could help her cope with this. It couldn't be Mother or Papa or even Alice or Lizzie. She tried to frame her confused thoughts into a sentence, but the day's events were too jumbled in her mind to make sense of them. Suddenly, Bernie realized that she needed to talk to Vincent. It wouldn't be the first time she had turned to him. She knew she could trust him to listen to her deepest secrets, even though she was ashamed of them. He would understand. Tomorrow she would ask Aunt Rose to drive her out to the Soldiers' Home.

21

NOVEMBER 1918 TO MARCH 1919
The Dinner Guest

Bernie and her family kept a close eye on Nick that fall and winter. They longed to see him laugh and join in the life around him. As months went by with little progress, they each worried secretly in their hearts but tried to stay cheerful for Nick and one another.

One evening after supper, as Bernie helped Mother clean up, she suggested a plan to help Nick. "Mother," she said, "I would like to invite a friend to have dinner at our house."

"Yes, dear, who is it?"

"It's Vincent. He's the soldier I visit at the Indiana State Soldiers' Home."

"Are you sure you want to do this?"

"I'm certain. He has become a very close friend of mine. I want him to meet my family."

Mother paused and put the cup she was drying on the kitchen table. "You're not. . . . " Mother said hesitantly, "You're not planning to do anything foolish, are you?"

"Whatever do you mean?" Bernie asked, knowing full-well what Mother meant.

Mother sat down on a kitchen chair. "When you first asked permission to go out to the Soldiers' Home, Papa and I were a bit—well, as a matter of fact, we were more than a bit—concerned that you might form an attachment to one of these young men."

"Do you want to know if I have a crush on Vincent?"

"Yes, that is exactly what I want to know. It is easy to become fond of unfortunate people who are in his position. We wouldn't want you to become involved romantically with someone just because you pity him."

Bernie was tempted to tease her mother by making her think that was indeed what she had in mind. Instead, she said, "Vincent is not the kind of person anyone should pity. It's true that I am very fond of him. But you can rest assured, I am not going to fall in love with him. In the first place, Vincent has a girlfriend back home. I might even want to ask her to dinner if she comes to visit him."

"That would be fine," Mother said, her face brightening with relief. "We'd be happy to meet her. Shall we wait until she comes? Then we can invite them both together?"

"I think it would be a better idea for Vincent to come now." Bernie waited a bit before she said, "I think Nick should meet him."

"I don't know," Mother said, turning back to dry the rest of the dishes. "It might be a bit soon. Having a wounded soldier here would just remind Nick of the terrible things that happened to him during the war."

"Nick has been home for several months now," Bernie said. "He stays in his room most of the time, with his curtains drawn. It's all we can do to coax him downstairs to eat a meal."

At first, Mother had insisted on taking a tray upstairs to Nick three times a day. She would load the tray with food that later had to be carried back downstairs, usually with little evidence that he had touched anything at all. After that, when he did come down and sit at the table, Nick fed most of his meal to Sheppie—until Papa put his foot down. The dog was no longer allowed to be inside the house during mealtime.

After leaving the table, Nick often went outside to sit silently on the porch. If he saw a neighbor approach the house, he got up and went back upstairs to his room. It was almost impossible to get him to engage in conversation. Bernie had tried with disastrous results one evening. She had joined him on the porch swing, even though it was far too chilly to sit outside.

She sat quietly beside her brother until she could stand the silence no longer and then handed him the letter Jack wrote. "Would you like to read it?"

He shook his head. She began to read it aloud. He stopped her. "I don't want to hear it."

"But you need to hear it." Bernie persisted. "Among other things, Jack wrote that it was his idea and not yours to run away and join the army. Why didn't you tell us? Why didn't you tell Mr. McClarty? Why are you being so stubborn?"

"You wouldn't understand."

"You might be surprised how understanding I can be. I learned a lot while you were gone."

Nick sat with his lips clamped together tightly before he said in a quiet voice. "Jack was my best friend. I was with him when he died. I didn't want anyone to know it was his idea to join the army. It seemed disloyal to his memory."

Bernie heard the pain in Nick's voice. She touched her brother's arm. "You were a good friend to him. I wish I had been."

Nick got up and started to go into the house. Bernie asked, "Is it okay if I show Jack's letter to Papa?"

He paused before answering, "Do what you think is right."

When Bernie told Vincent about this conversation and asked what he thought she should do, he replied in almost the same words Nick had used. That was when the thought occurred to her that he and Nick might have something in common.

That was why Bernie now pressed Mother to invite Vincent to come for dinner. "I think Vincent might help Nick find his way back to us. Vincent knows what Nick went through on the battlefield."

Mother didn't answer right away. She went over to the window and gazed outside for a while before saying, "You may be right."

"It's worth a try," Bernie said. She walked over to the window and hugged her mother.

Even though Mother had doubts about inviting Vincent to dinner, Bernie was proud of the way she had handled the situation. Ever the gracious hostess, Mother took her prized embroidered tablecloth and napkins from the cedar chest and put them on the table. Mother set out her best china and silverware. She called Aunt Lolly at the farm to see if there were any early daffodils in bloom. Mother was able to fill a crystal vase for the center of the table.

Bernie surveyed the scene. "Mother, everything is lovely, but you do remember that Vincent has very little eyesight. He probably won't see much of it."

"Perhaps not, but then again perhaps he will appreciate it. He can smell the flowers. He can touch the china and silverware. As your Grandmother Epperson says, 'Quality things feel better to the touch.'"

Bernie began to feel nervous as Aunt Rose drove her out to the Soldiers' Home to get Vincent. What if Nick refused to come downstairs? He had behaved so terribly on November 11th when the Armistice, or ceasefire, had been announced. Everyone else was so jubilant. Church bells rang out all over town at 11 o'clock in the morning. People poured out into the streets waving flags to celebrate the end of the war. Bernie had been wild to be part of it. After school, she had knocked on Nick's door.

He had growled, "You go on and celebrate the end of the 'war to end all wars,' but leave me out of it."

Remembering his attitude that day, Bernie asked, "What if Nick refuses to come down? Or, what if he comes down and is rude to Vincent?" She remembered her very first meeting with Vincent and what a struggle it had been for her to get through to him.

"It will be all right," Aunt Rose said. "No matter what happens this evening, Vincent will understand."

By now, the bandages were off of Vincent's eyes. Although he still could not see much, he could get around fairly well with the aid of his cane. Bernie had learned how to assist him with his walking. She bent her arm, and he slipped his hand under it as they made their way out to the auto where Aunt Rose was waiting.

"I'm looking forward to a good home-cooked meal," he said.

"I promise you the food will be good, but as I told you, I don't know what to expect from Nick. My brother has been less than pleasant lately."

"It's all right," Vincent reassured her. "I've been through that myself. I just hope I don't upset your folks too much. Eating with the men at the Home is one thing. Table manners don't count for much there. I hope I don't make a mess of things."

Once inside the Epperson dining room, Bernie knew that Vincent had made a positive impression on Papa with his gentlemanly ways. It soon became evident that he had charmed Mother as well. Vincent took a deep breath and said, "The daffodils smell wonderful, Mrs. Epperson. They remind me of home. Are you a gardener?" Mother admitted she got them from the farm and then went twittering happily into the kitchen to check on the roast beef.

Bernie didn't know how he did it, but Ben had managed to convince Nick to join them at the dinner table. She sighed with relief when she saw that her brother had shaved and was wearing a decent shirt and jacket. He took the seat next to Vincent. Bernie tried her best not to stare at the two of them together. As she bowed her head for Papa's prayer, she added a silent one of her own that the evening would go well.

Vincent ran his fingers lightly over the raised pattern on the linen napkin and wanted to know who had done such fine embroidery. Bernie couldn't stop grinning with pleasure. After that the conversation flowed easily. Even Nick managed to add a few words now and then.

"Where are you from, young man?" Papa wanted to know. When Vincent replied that he had grown up in a small farming community just south of Indianapolis, Papa wanted to know if Vincent knew a certain friend of his. He didn't, but he did remember when his high school basketball team had played the school here in town.

"That was a few years before my time, but I think we beat you," Nick said.

Vincent replied, "There is always next year."

COLLECTIONS OF THE ALLEN COUNTY–FORT WAYNE HISTORICAL SOCIETY

By definition an armistice is a temporary halt in fighting, a cease-fire. At 11 a.m. on the eleventh day of the eleventh month in 1918 the final armistice was announced, effectively ending World War I, which at the time was known as the war to end all wars. When people found out about the armistice, celebrations broke out in the early hours of the morning and continued all day. The Treaty of Versailles, signed on June 28, 1919, in France formally ended the war.

Bernie exchanged pleased glances with Aunt Rose. Nobody seemed distressed when Vincent needed help buttering his roll and accidentally stuck his fingers in his mashed potatoes.

After the meal, Bernie could not have been more pleased when Nick asked Vincent if he would like to go outside, despite the cold early spring night, and sit on the front porch. She would have given anything to go out with them and listen to their conversation. She started to follow them, but Mother looked at her with that old familiar warning expression that needed no words. Even Aunt Rose held Bernie's arm and shook her head. "I think maybe those two have things to talk about that might not be said if they thought anyone else was listening."

Bernie knew that Mother and Aunt Rose were right. After all she had invited Vincent so that he could get acquainted with Nick. So, she stayed inside to help clear the table and do the dishes. Papa went into the parlor. Now that the war was over, newspapers were allowed in the house once again.

Back in the kitchen, Mother sighed and laughed, "Women's work. Will it ever change?"

American women continued to fight for suffrage throughout World War I and after the final armistice in 1918.

"It will if Bernie and I have anything to do about it," Aunt Rose replied.

Mother looked thoughtful. "I suppose you and the Lafayette Franchise League are back at work now that the war is over."

"We never stopped. We're trying to get an amendment to the U.S. Constitution. We can always use more help," Aunt Rose said, looking squarely in Mother's direction.

"I'll give it some thought," Mother smiled as she answered.

22

Surprises

Bernie and Lizzie walked through the halls of the high school on their way to the principal's office. Neither of them spoke. Bernie's mouth was so dry that she could not have uttered a word even if she had tried. She supposed that Lizzie was every bit as nervous as she was. This was the day that both of them had looked forward to all year—and yet dreaded. With graduation only weeks away, this was the day that the senior class standings would be posted. "You go first," Bernie said to Lizzie.

Lizzie hesitated, squared her shoulders and stepped forward. She stood looking at the list for a few moments and did not say a word when she turned back to face Bernie.

Bernie swallowed hard and then walked to the bulletin board. There at the top of the list was the name of the person who had the best grades for the past four years of school. This was the person who would be the class valedictorian. Bernie stared at the list with disbelief. The first name was Elizabeth C. Mifflin. Lizzie had won. She would make the main speech, as Alice had done a few years earlier. Lizzie, not Bernie, would stand up on stage in front of everyone to be honored.

Bernie's eyes moved down to the second place. When she saw the name listed there she felt sick to her stomach. She covered her mouth with her hand. It was not her name on that line. Bernice R. Epperson was listed at number three. She could barely force herself to turn around and look at her cousin. She knew what words she needed to say, but how could she say them? She remembered how Lizzie had reacted when the winner of the Lafayette Franchise League Essay Contest had been announced a few years before. Lizzie had seemed genuinely glad for Bernie, even though she had wanted to win. This kind of generosity was one of the things that Bernie loved so much about her cousin.

Bernie moved toward Lizzie and hugged her. She started to say, "Congratulations." But before she could say a word, Lizzie burst out with, "Oh, Bernie. I'm so sorry. I can't bear for you to be disappointed. I'm sure you could make a much better speech than I'll be able to do."

Bernie and Lizzie's graduation outfits would have looked similar to the ones worn in this photograph of a high school graduating class of 1918 in Marion, Indiana. Education had recently undergone extensive reforms in Indiana and across the United States. In 1910 high school graduation rates were around 10 percent. By 1920, when Bernie graduated, the graduation rate had doubled. Statistically, women had higher graduation rates than men at this time, which is evident in the photograph.

Swallowing her pride, Bernie replied, "No, truly—I'm so happy for you, Lizzie. You're going to do fine. I know your speech will make us all proud. And, it will be something for Peggy and Susie to live up to."

The principal had stepped out of his office to witness the scene. "I'm glad to see that you two girls are still friends."

"We always have been," Bernie said. "Besides, we're cousins, so we've kept the honor in the family."

The principal continued, "I just want you to know that this was the closest the scores have ever been. The top three students were within a few grade points of each other. All three of you are to be congratulated."

It was cold comfort, but Bernie knew she would have to learn to live with it. She could do her crying at home tonight. When she told Vincent about Lizzie winning the prize she had wanted so badly, he answered, "Yes, you feel bad about this right now, but in a strange way setbacks can make you stronger."

At first her feelings were bruised by his seeming dismissal of her disappointment. But, after she thought about it a little while, she realized how foolish and shallow she must seem to let something like that get her down. Vincent had faced a lot worse than she had. In fact, a lot of the people she met at the Soldiers' Home had shown her what real courage was.

Bernie had been so happy to have both of her brothers safely home and the war over, but things were no longer the same as they had been before the war. Strange, how when she was younger she used to think that she would give anything not to be teased by Ben and Nick. Now she missed it. She would have preferred the teasing banter in place of the sense of uneasiness in the air. She didn't know what to do about it.

Nick had been quiet and uncommunicative since he came home from the war. Mother worried about his leg. She warned him not to overdo it on the long walks he took with Vincent and Sheppie. Nick snapped that the doctor had said he needed to exercise his leg so that it did not stiffen up.

Ben made no secret that he was unhappy working at the store. He wanted to be anywhere else but at Epperson's Emporium. That made Papa unhappy. When Papa was unhappy, Mother was unhappy. That made everyone unhappy.

Talking about this with Vincent had shown Bernie that there was no wishing things were the way they used to be. It was better to look forward and not back. He had said, "When I'm upset, I just try to get busy doing something."

Apparently, Vincent had taught them all a lot of things. One day after Nick returned from a long walk with Vincent, he and Ben drove their new friend back to the Soldiers' Home. They were gone for an unusually long time and arrived home late for supper. Mother had been pacing between the table and the window, fussing about how the food was getting cold. When they came in at last and took their places, they each muttered a brief, "Sorry." Nothing else was said except the quick blessing of the food. They were too old to be scolded now, but Papa's demeanor made it clear how he felt.

At the end of a very silent meal, Nick announced, "I have something to tell you."

Bernie felt the tension growing in the room. She had noticed Nick and Ben exchanging furtive glances.

Nick continued, "As a matter of fact, both Ben and I have something to tell you."

Everyone stopped eating and looked from boy to boy—or rather, from young man to young man.

Nick said, "I have decided that I would like to go back to school. I've always been good at mathematics. I want to take a few classes and then work at the store with you, Papa."

Papa was obviously surprised by this announcement.

Nick continued, "Then, if it works out for both of us, we can repaint the store sign to say "Epperson and Son" again—like it was when you worked for your father."

It took a while for Papa to take this in.

The second part of the announcement was even more of a shock. Nick looked at Ben, who said, "Go ahead. Tell the rest of it." With Ben's encouragement, Nick continued, "Ben and I have talked this out. When I go to work at the store, this will allow Ben to do what he has always wanted to do. He can go west with his camera."

Papa started to interrupt, but Mother reached over and put a calming hand on Papa's arm. She looked at Papa and nodded slightly. She hadn't said a word, but it was enough for Papa to realize that he was outnumbered.

Bernie could not help but wonder if Papa remembered Aunt Rose and her lost opportunity to go west with the man she loved. Did he also remember how he had stood up to his own father when he wanted to marry Mother? Bernie thought it must be very difficult to allow your children to make their own choices.

Papa sat quietly. The longer he sat the more his tired face began to relax. Before the table was cleared, Papa managed to look happy. He and Nick began

General stores of the early twentieth century were somewhat similar to the big box stores of today. They carried a variety of goods such as clothing, fabric, and linens. Unlike today, stores were not self-serve. Instead a customer was always assisted by an employee. Bernie's father's store, Epperson's Emporium, may have looked similar to this midwestern clothing and dry goods store, ca. 1910–1919.

to talk about what duties Nick would take over at the store. Papa even asked Ben if he had made any travel arrangements.

A strange feeling of peace seemed to settle over the family. Things certainly weren't as they had been before the war, and Bernie now knew that they could never go back—too much had happened. But she smiled as she watched her father and her two brothers talking earnestly together—as men. It felt good to see them making plans. Maybe change was not such a bad thing after all.

23

Stepping Out

There was to be a picnic to celebrate Bernie's eighteenth birthday, so the Epperson family piled into the car and headed for the Mifflin farm. As Papa turned onto the long lane that went to the farm they saw a bizarre sight ahead of them. Alice was galloping along like a young colt, her red curly mane flying loose in the breeze.

"Won't that girl ever grow up and act like a lady?" Papa snorted.

Ben laughed, "What would be the point of that? Alice acting like a lady wouldn't be Alice."

As they drew nearer they could see that she was running alongside a young man who was pushing a wheelbarrow. In the wheelbarrow were two children hanging on for dear life and shrieking happily at the top of their lungs. Alice's three younger sisters followed closely behind, laughing as they ran.

"Whoever is that?" Papa asked.

"I think those are Emily Kennedy's children. You know, Jack's sister," Mother said. "Lolly has taken them under her wing again."

"But who is that pushing the wheelbarrow?" Papa insisted.

An eerie feeling crept along Bernie's spine, as she stared at the back of the young man. She remembered vividly that day, near the end of the war, when Nick had returned home unexpectedly. For a moment she had a wild fantasy that Jack had come home. What if the past couple of years had been a horrible dream or a mistake? Maybe Jack hadn't died in France.

As the Hupmobile drew nearer, Papa honked the horn with a loud ca-doo-gah sound. The young man stopped and stood at the side of the roadway. He turned and waved at them as they went past.

Of course, it wasn't Jack, but Bernie was shaken by the thought. As they passed him on her side of the car, she couldn't help but notice his eyes. They were the most astonishing deep-blue color she had ever seen. She put one hand to her chest. She felt the cobalt blue bead on the fishing line that she wore beneath her blouse, where no one would see it.

"I don't think we know that young man," Mother said.

"Well, I've seen him somewhere," Nick said. "I'm sure of it."

"Probably Alice's latest beau," Ben suggested.

As soon as Papa stopped the Hupmobile in front of the farmhouse, Lizzie and her younger sisters ran toward them and jumped up on the running boards, making it impossible for anyone to open the car doors and get out. Lizzie, who still couldn't keep a secret if her life depended on it, was bubbling over, anxious to share everything she knew.

With her audience trapped inside the car, Lizzie burst out, "Oh, Bernie, you will never believe what happened! It was so exciting. Yesterday afternoon we heard an airplane pass over our house. It was flying quite low. We all ran out to wave. Then we heard the plane's engine begin to sputter and cough. There were little puffs of smoke coming out of the engine."

By this time, Susie and Peggy had joined in the conversation.

"We were sure it was going to crash," said Susie.

"Father ran to get our auto, and we followed it," Peggy continued.

"The plane landed in the meadow just beyond the pond," Susie said.

"The pilot climbed out," said Lizzie. "And, he's been here ever since."

Nick, who had been listening intently, replied, "Now I know where I've seen him. There are posters up all over town with his picture on them. He's a barnstormer."

"What in the world is that?" Mother asked.

Nick described how these men, who had been pilots during the war, were now traveling all over the country giving demonstrations of fancy flying. They flew upside down, made loops, barrel rolls, and more. "Barnstormers," he said, "come to small towns alone or in small troops and offer locals a chance to fly with them for a fee."

Lizzie interjected, "Well, my father could hardly wait to get his hands on that plane to find out what was wrong with it. He and Philip, that's the pilot's name, tinkered with the engine until Mama made them both come inside for dinner. They gobbled their food and went right back out until dark when they couldn't see to work anymore. Father is in seventh heaven to have an airplane to work on."

Susie said, "Mama told Philip he must stay with us because we have plenty of room. You know how Mama is."

They all nodded. Papa muttered under his breath, "Haven't I always said she takes in every stray that shows up on her doorstep. Now she has one that dropped out of the sky."

By this time, Alice and Philip had made their way to the Epperson automobile.

"This is Philip Fairfield," Alice announced.

He reached out to shake hands with Papa, Ben, and Nick. He took off his cap and nodded politely toward Mother and said, "Pleased to meet you, Ma'am."

Susie and Peggy jumped from the auto's running board and buzzed about Philip like honey bees in spring flowers. To Bernie's surprise Philip opened the car door on her side and offered his arm to help her down. Once again she looked into those hypnotic blue eyes and her cheeks grew embarrassingly

MARTIN'S PHOTO SHOP COLLECTION, INDIANA HISTORICAL SOCIETY

Barnstorming became popular after World War I when pilots from the war returned home and wanted to continue flying to make a living. Many were able to buy planes inexpensively because the federal government was selling its surplus Curtiss JN-4 "Jenny" biplanes for as little as $200. Barnstormers were either individual pilots or troops of pilots that came into small rural towns, putting on daredevil aerial shows and giving rides for a fee.

warm. She tried to pull away, but he held on for a few seconds and said, "This must be the birthday girl."

Then he turned from her and lifted little Mazie Kennedy from the wheelbarrow. She clung to him. No amount of coaxing could pry her away. He hoisted her brother, Georgie, onto his broad shoulders and walked to where a long trestle table sat beneath the shady maples near the farmhouse. Bernie watched while Mazie climbed up on a chair and insisted that Philip sit next to her. As he sat down, Philip put Georgie down on his other side.

"Guest of honor at the end of the table," Aunt Lolly directed Bernie, and everyone else began to take their places. After the prayer, the family passed around heaps of food in large bowls and platters. Bernie tried to busy herself with these, but occasionally she glanced up to sneak another look at the fascinating guest. Each time she did, she saw that he was looking back at her.

After they ate, Mother suggested that Bernie open her presents before cutting the cake. "I think we need time for our food to settle."

Everyone agreed. They moved the dishes away from Bernie and brought their gifts, forming a tall stack on the table in front of her. There were so many that she could not even see over them.

"Now, this is a welcome surprise," Nick said. "Ben and I have been trying for years to make our little sister disappear."

Bernie stood up hurriedly so that she could see all of them gathered around the table. "You didn't think it would be that easy, did you?" As she said this she looked fondly at Nick, who was displaying a boyish grin that no one had seen in a long time. She didn't mind hearing a good-natured gibe from him. In fact, she welcomed it and any other indication that her brother was finally making his way back from the dark place where he had been for so long.

"Open our present first," called little Mazie. "Mother made it especially for you."

Not to be outdone by his younger sister, Georgie added, "It's a hat." Everyone laughed at his revelation.

Bernie lifted the creation from its box. It was made of warm golden straw and decorated with white daisies and a mint green ribbon. "It is just beautiful," Bernie said.

"Let's see how you look with it on," Aunt Lolly suggested.

Emily got up and came to place it on Bernie's head. As she did so, Bernie remembered that time so long ago when she had first seen Emily and had made a disparaging remark about her shabby hat. Now, with Aunt Lolly's help, Emily had a thriving millinery shop and was in demand by some of the richest women in town.

Bernie reached out and hugged Emily as Ben snapped a picture of them with his new camera. "You have no idea how much this hat means to me. Thank you," Bernie said.

The next gift was from Ben. It was a large photo album in which he had placed portraits that he had made of each member of the family. Bernie said, "I hope there is plenty of room for me to put in all the beautiful pictures you are going to send me from out West."

There was a small box from Aunt Rose. When Bernie opened it, she gasped. On a bed of white cotton lay the delicate miniature portrait that Aunt Rose's beau from long ago had painted. "Are you certain you want to give me this? It is such a treasure."

"I have no daughter of my own to give it to. I want very much for you to have it to remember me by."

"I already have so much to remember you by," Bernie said, trying not to cry when she recalled all the wonderful adventures she had shared with Aunt Rose. She thought about the trip to Washington, DC, and visiting veterans at the Soldiers' Home. She also thought about the secrets she and Aunt Rose shared. Even the latest secret that included Ben. Aunt Rose had written to her old love to tell him that her nephew wanted to travel west. Her friend had responded that he would be more than happy to show Ben some exciting places to photograph.

Nick's gift saved Bernie from breaking down and crying in front of everyone. As she removed the wrappings, he said, "When I saw this book I thought of you."

"What is it?" Alice wanted to know.

Bernie passed it down the table so everyone could see the title: *Ten Days in a Mad-House.*

"It's by your favorite author," Nick added, "Nellie Bly."

Papa said, "Speaking of Nellie Bly," he paused meaningfully. "I have learned who she is—a commendable woman who makes her living by writing. I think it's time you opened the present from your mother and me." It took a bit of effort to get the wrappings off the large box that contained, to Bernie's amazement, a typing machine.

Pictured here is Indiana Governor James P. Goodrich signing the document ratifying the Nineteenth Amendment to the U.S. Constitution on January 16, 1920. Eight months later on August 18, 1920, Tennessee was the thirty-sixth state to ratify the amendment. At this point, three-fourths of the states had ratified it, meaning it could finally become law. On August 26, 1920, Secretary of State Bainbridge Colby certified the ratification. American women finally had the right to vote in federal elections.

"Now, you can type your college papers and your news stories. It will be interesting to see how much trouble you can get into that way." Somehow she knew that this was Papa's way of saying he was proud of her.

The last gift was from the Mifflins. It was a beautiful gold watch that she could pin on her dress.

"We found it in an old trunk that had belonged to Grandma Mifflin," Alice said.

"And Father managed to get it working again," Lizzie added.

"And we helped polish it," Susie and Peggy said, not wanting to be left out.

Bernie stood and looked at everyone gathered around the table. "Thank you for these wonderful gifts. I will treasure them. But the best gift of all is my family. I cannot tell you how much I love each one of you."

After the table was cleared and the food put away, Aunt Lolly brought out the cake. She placed it in front of Bernie saying, "Your birthday has come on a day we've been working toward for years." Bernie, Aunt Rose, Alice, and her sisters had a pretty good idea of what Lolly was going to say next and felt excited and nervous all at once. Aunt Lolly continued, "August 18, 1920, will long be remembered as the day the Nineteenth Amendment to the United States Constitution was ratified, giving women the right to vote." A cheer went up around the table.

Papa spoke up, "That poses a bit of a problem, doesn't it?"

"What do you mean?" Bernie wanted to know.

"Whatever will you ladies do with your time now that there is no longer any need for the Lafayette Franchise League?"

"Haven't you heard the old saying that a woman's work is never done? We have a new organization that will keep us busy," Aunt Lolly said.

Alice explained, "It's called the League of Women Voters."

"Well, what's the purpose of that?" Papa asked. He seemed genuinely interested, not at all like he had reacted when Bernie first became involved with the suffrage movement. Maybe she and her aunts and cousins had changed his mind about women voting.

"The members will study the issues and the candidates in order to prepare women to vote intelligently," Lizzie explained. "One of the criticisms of allowing women to vote was that they would simply do what their menfolk told them to do."

"I intend to be a part of the League of Women Voters, Papa," Bernie announced.

"You won't be old enough to vote until you're twenty-one," Papa reminded her.

"But I can vote this year," Mother interrupted. "And, I'm going to join the League of Women Voters so that I will understand exactly what I am voting for and not have to depend upon any man to tell me."

Bernie thought Papa looked as though he had been hit by a bolt of lightning.

"Furthermore," Mother added, "Bernie has convinced me that I should take lessons and learn how to drive the Hupmobile."

The League of Women Voters was organized by Carrie Chapman Catt in 1920. Catt had previously been the president of the National American Woman Suffrage Association, the organization to which the Lafayette Franchise League belonged. While the League of Women Voters would fight for many social issues in the future, its underlying mission was to encourage women to vote, a mission it continues today.

Papa, who had just started to take a bite of Bernie's birthday cake, lowered his fork. "I wonder," he said, "if there will ever come a time when I can stop asking myself what in the world she will do next."

"Oh, Papa," Bernie grinned. "You should know, after all these years, that you will always be wondering what I will do next."

"This time I wasn't thinking about you, Bernie. I was talking about your mother."

Everyone roared with laughter, especially Papa, who laughed the loudest.

As people stood to clear the table after they had their fill of cake, Bernie was surprised to see Philip head in her direction. She felt a faint flutter of excitement inside her chest when he said, "I seem to be the only one who didn't have anything to give you for your birthday."

She managed to reply smoothly, "I don't need anything else. It has been a perfect day."

"But I really would like to give you something. Just name it."

Bernie answered him boldly, "Very well, then. You can take me for a ride in your aeroplane."

Bernie caught a glimpse of Papa, who was standing close enough to overhear their conversation. He had a startled look on his face. He started to say something but quickly closed his mouth.

Philip said with an exaggerated bow, "Your wish is my command, but do you want to ask your parents if it's okay with them? I don't want them to be worried about your safety."

Bernie paused for only a second before saying, "I am certain that if my Uncle Leroy helped you repair your plane, there is nothing for anyone to worry about."

Ben had also overheard and added, "You'll probably be a lot safer than you were the day you tried to help Nick, Jack, and me fly the plane we built in McClarty's barn."

Philip looked at Bernie quizzically. She said, "That's a long story. I'll tell you later."

"Well then, what are we waiting for? Let's go."

"Isn't it a bit late in the day for this?" Bernie asked.

"As a matter of fact, this is my favorite time for flying. I think we are going to have a beautiful sunset. You'll get a view of the world that you will never forget. You're going to love flying."

Somehow, Bernie knew that Philip had spoken more truth than he could imagine. Today she was eighteen and she was certain that a lifetime of exciting things lay ahead on her horizon. As Philip took her arm and helped her climb into the plane, Bernie thought that Papa would do well to wonder what in the world *she* would do next.

Afterword

Giant Steps is a work of fiction. Most people think of fiction as something that never happened, but I like to define historical fiction as a "truth story." Writing a novel is serious business. For one thing, it may be the only insight into a given era that will be available to the reader. Therefore, it should be as correct as possible. This was especially important to me because Bernie was born the same year as my mother. She grew up and attended school in the story during the same time my mother had grown up, so I had the benefit of my mother's school-day memories.

I am often asked if my books are autobiographical. In a way they are because they often reflect my hopes, dreams, and aspirations. Occasionally, I make use of an incident that actually happened to me. For instance, I still blush when I recall the time I dropped the offering plate in church and the coins bouncing about on the wooden floor created quite a racket. This embarrassment became part of *Giant Steps* during the scene in which Nick and Ben made fun of Bernie for having dropped the offering plate in their church.

Although the characters in the story are fictional, some are based on real persons. Others are composites of many persons, and some stand for types of persons. Bernie and her brothers, Ben and Nick, as well as their friend, Jack, were typical of many individuals of the period. Their lives illustrate the double standard of behavior expected of young people at the time. Girls were expected to act one way and boys another.

Change was certainly a very real part of *Giant Steps*. Jack's father, who was a blacksmith, was fighting a losing battle against mechanization. As trains, streetcars, and autos came into common use, his services as a blacksmith were becoming obsolete. In some ways his experience was not much different from people today who are having a difficult time because of changes brought about by new technology. Our world was and is changing. Jobs that were once common in a community have altered extremely or disappeared. For example, in the time period of *Giant Steps*, newspapers were the major form of news transmission. Today, however, newspapers are struggling and changing drastically to survive the challenges of television and the Internet.

Some of the places depicted in the story are actual places as well. The Wabash River divides Lafayette and West Lafayette just as it did a hundred years ago. Descriptions of the town square, where Epperson's Emporium did

Indiana State Soldiers Home, La Fayette, Ind.

Bernie's veteran friend, Vincent, was in the hospital building at the Indiana State Soldiers' Home in Lafayette, Indiana, when she first met him. As he progressed in his rehabilitation, he may have stayed in the men's building, pictured here.

business, are also accurate. Although the Epperson store is fictional, stores such as this did exist at that time in communities such as Lafayette.

The site of the old fort on the river, where Bernie and her cousins Alice and Lizzie beat the boys to a picnic spot is a real place. A pioneer named Sandford Cox described how children in the 1800s found beads in the grass there. It is possible to visit this place today, although the beads that voyageurs traded there with Native Americans are long gone.

Another place that really existed during World War I is the Indiana State Soldiers' Home in Lafayette. It opened in 1896 for veterans of the Civil War. After serving generations of veterans, it still provides medical care and housing today and is known as the Indiana Veterans' Home.

The major events portrayed in *Giant Steps* are part of history. Nick's running away to become a soldier at age sixteen (and misrepresenting his age) and Ben's joining up and then getting the flu and nearly dying were based on real situations that happened to real persons. Many young men left home and signed up to join the armed services during World War I, some of them underage. There are examples from my family. My father and uncles were soldiers in World War I. Thousands of soldiers became sick with influenza, and many of them died. One of my uncles was a flu survivor.

Barnstorming pilots are also part of the historical record. Many of them learned to fly while serving their country. Philip Fairfield, the barnstorming pilot whom Bernie met at her birthday party, was inspired by the many men who came home from the war and earned their living by putting on air shows.

Most important, the struggle of women to get the vote was all too real. Women and girls marched in Washington, DC, just as Bernie and her family members did. Many women were actually ridiculed, and some were jailed throughout the long years of the suffragette movement. The division within many women's suffrage organizations was also real. Not everyone agreed on what to do; this was especially true when World War I came along. Many suffragettes wondered where their efforts would be most effective. Many, like Bernie, were torn between helping and supporting their fathers, brothers, uncles, and cousins or continuing to fight to get women the vote.

British women were also very active in winning the vote for women in their country. The guest speaker, Isabel Grandison, who talked to the Lafayette Franchise League, was a fictional composite of women from England who visited the United States to share their struggle with American suffragettes. The 2015 motion picture *Suffragette* chronicles some events that happened in England during their fight for the vote.

In 1920 there were forty-eight states, and it took three-fourths of these, or thirty-six, to ratify the Nineteenth Amendment. This took place on August 18 of that year. However, it also meant that a dozen states still rejected the right to vote for women. It was not until 1984 that Mississippi ratified the amendment, the last state to do so.

Aunt Lolly was correct when she said that women's work is never done. Getting the vote, although it was a positive step forward, did not solve all the inequities women faced. There was still a long way to go. In December 2015 in the U.S. Congress there were only 88 women in the 441-member House of Representatives. There were 100 senators, but only 20 were female.

There are still issues in the workplace. In 2015 studies showed that a woman was the chief breadwinner in four out of ten households in the United States with children under the age of eighteen. Yet, women are often paid less than men who are doing the same job. Unfortunately, women who are abused and poor, similar to the fictional Edna Shmidt and her granddaughter in *Giant Steps*, could be found in many communities during the last century and are still with us today.

Yes, women's AND men's work is never done. For no one can be equal until everyone is treated equally.

Acknowledgments

Almost any published author, if she or he is honest about it, will admit that help is needed from many sources. This is especially true of a work set in an historical time period. I am especially appreciative of my Indiana Historical Society Press editor and longtime friend, Teresa Baer. She encourages me when I am ready to "throw in the towel" on certain projects. Everyone needs a cheerleader.

I am grateful to those persons who carefully researched references to make sure they are correct. Such things as descriptions of clothing, food, daily life, language, etc., must be in proper context. Quotes from newspaper articles had to be verified and documented. When I wrote the speech given by the English visitor, I wanted to use a certain quote. Researchers discovered, however, that while the quote was accurate, it was not said until ten years after the speech in the book was supposed to have been given. Therefore, it had to be cut out, much to my dismay. Historical pictures had to be found to illustrate events in the book. I want to thank IHS Press intern Stephanie Schulze, who helped make *Giant Steps* a truth story. I also want to thank Chelsea Sutton, IHS Press contract editor, who did the first round of editing and helped to make sure the timeline was correct throughout the book.

Stories of Heroic and Pioneering Women

Atwood, Kathryn J. *Women Heroes of World War I: Sixteen Remarkable Resisters, Soldiers, Spies, and Medics*. Chicago Review Press, 2014. In this book, Atwood tells the stories of the wartime exploits of sixteen women from the United States, Europe, and Australia.

Bank, Mirra. *Anonymous Was a Woman: A Celebration in Words and Images of Traditional American Art and the Women Who Made It*. New York: Saint Martin's Press, 1979. Collection of American folk art by ordinary women of the eighteenth and nineteenth centuries, including reproductions of samplers, quilts, paintings, and needle-pictures along with excerpts from diaries and letters, sampler verse, books, and magazines of the period.

Boomhower, Ray E. *Fighting For Equality: A Life of May Wright Sewall*. Indianapolis: IHS Press, 2007. Sewall was an educator, woman's rights advocate, and peace activist in central Indiana from 1871 until her death in 1920.

Macy, Sue. *Bylines: A Photobiography of Nellie Bly*. Washington, DC: National Geographic Children's Books, 2009. This is a photographic biography of the great woman journalist and advocate for women's rights.

Marlow, Joyce, ed. *Votes for Women: The Virago Book of Suffragettes*. London: Virago Press, 2001. Collection of documents, speeches, journals, and extracts from books and letters relating to the women's movement from 1870 to 1928 in England.

Sheen, Barbara. *Janet Guthrie: Indy Car Racing Pioneer*. Farmington Hills, MI: KidHaven Press, 2010. Guthrie was the first woman to compete in the Indianapolis 500 race.

Sherr, Lynn. *Sally Ride: America's First Woman in Space*. New York: Simon and Schuster, 2015. Biography of America's first woman astronaut and first woman in space.

Smith, Norma. *Jeanette Rankin: America's Conscience*. Helena: Montana Historical Society Press, 2002. Rankin was the first woman member of the U.S. Congress.

Smith–Daugherty, Rhonda. *Jacqueline Cochran: Biography of a Pioneer Aviator*. Jefferson, NC: McFarland, 2012. Biography of Jacqueline Cochran, first female aviator to win the Bendix Air Race, to fly a bomber, to break the speed of sound, and to participate in astronaut training.

Theoharis, Jeanne. *The Rebellious Life of Mrs. Rosa Parks*. Boston: Beacon Press, 2013. Rosa Parks is often portrayed as a weary woman who was arrested for sitting in the wrong section of a bus in a segregated society. Actually, she had been a civil-rights activist before her act of protest and she continued to fight for equal rights for African Americans the rest of her life.

Wilson, Dorothy Clarke. *Lone Woman: The Story of Elizabeth Blackwell, the First Woman Doctor*. Boston: Little, Brown, and Company, 1970. Blackwell established women's place in medicine in the United States and England during the nineteenth century.

Yousafzai, Malala, and Christina Lamb. *I Am Malala: The Girl Who Stood Up for Education and Was Shot by the Taliban*. Young Readers Ed. New York: Little, Brown, and Company, 2013. Malala Yousafzai was a teenage girl from Pakistan in 2012 when she was shot because she wanted to get an education, although girls were banned from schools at the time. After her recovery in Great Britain, she wrote this book with a British journalist and was the youngest recipient of the Nobel Peace Prize in 2014. She continues to speak out on behalf of education for girls worldwide.

Glossary

anesthetic: A substance that produces loss of sensation with or without loss of consciousness.

archaeologist: A person who studies fossils and material remains of past human life and activity.

armistice: A temporary suspension of hostilities between opponents.

artillery: Weapons that discharge missiles, such as bows and guns.

barnstormer: A pilot who tours through rural districts to take passengers for plane rides and/or to perform aerial stunts. Barnstorming was especially popular after World War I.

beau: Boyfriend.

blacksmith: A person who shapes metal objects using fire and/or a hammer in order to make items such as horseshoes and tools.

brocade: A rich silk fabric with a raised pattern in gold or silver.

brooding hen: A chicken who is sitting on her eggs.

carte de visite: A small photograph mounted on a card.

cheshire cat: A grinning cat that made its first appearance in the book *Alice's Adventures in Wonderland* by Lewis Carroll.

comeuppance: A deserved reprimand or punishment.

czar: An emperor of Russia before the 1917 revolution; also known as *tsar*.

damsel: An old expression for a young, unmarried woman.

dime novel: A paperback novel, often with a western theme, which generally costed ten cents. Dime novels were popular from the mid-nineteenth to early twentieth centuries.

discernment: The ability to understand shades of meaning or subtle differences between similar things.

disconcerting: Something that causes confusion and sometimes embarrassment.

emigrate: The act of leaving one's place of residence or country to live elsewhere.

epidemic: An outbreak of a disease that affects a large proportion of people within a population, community, or region.

Equal Rights Amendment: The Equal Rights Amendment (ERA) was written in 1923 by Alice Paul to ensure equality in all aspects of the law regardless of sex. The amendment has never been passed. The last state to ratify the ERA was Indiana in 1977.

fingerling fish: A young or small fish.

flivver: Slang term for a small, inexpensive, and sometimes old automobile.

franchise: A constitutional right or privilege, generally used in referencing the right to vote. See *suffrage*.

front: The furthest line that armed forces have reached and where the enemy may be engaged.

haymow: A place where hay is stored in a barn; also known as a hayloft.

hijinks: Boisterous, carefree antics or horseplay.

Hun: A derogatory, or disrespectful, name for Germans used during the world wars.

immigrate: The act of arriving and becoming established in a foreign country.

impetuous: A person who acts quickly without thought or care.

interurban: A type of electric railway that transported people within and between cities and towns on streetcars.

itinerant: To travel from place to place.

jury: A group of people sworn to give a verdict on a legal matter, such as for a criminal case.

lackey: Someone who does menial tasks or runs errands for another.

League of Women Voters: Founded in 1920 by Carrie Chapman Catt to help women learn about political and social issues and how to vote. The organization still exists to improve government and increase citizen engagement in politics.

middy blouse: A loose fitting blouse with a sailor collar worn by women and children.

millinery: Shop where a milliner, or hat maker, sells hats.

mohair: The yarn or fabric made from an Angora goat.

National American Woman Suffrage Association: The suffrage association that resulted from a merger between Elizabeth Cady Stanton and Susan B. Anthony's National Woman Suffrage Association and the American Woman Suffrage Association, founded in 1869 by Lucy Stone, Henry B. Blackwell, Julia Ward Howe, and others.

National Woman Suffrage Association (NWSA): The organization founded by Elizabeth Cady Stanton and Susan B. Anthony in 1869 that worked for women to have the right to vote.

oak apples: Large galls, or growths, on oak leaves or twigs produced by a gall wasp.

ominous: Foreshadowing danger or evil.

omission: Something neglected or left undone.

pandemic: An occurrence, such as the influenza outbreak, that affects a large proportion of people across a wide geographical area.

parliament: The highest legislative body in some democratic countries, such as the House of Commons in Great Britain.

party line: Unlike today, telephone conversations in the early twentieth century were not private. Several households often shared a line. It was not unusual for more than one person to listen to their neighbor's phone calls.

paste wax: A type of cleaner that can be used on hardwood floors, vehicles, and other surfaces.

phosphate soda: A tangy or sour beverage often made with fruit or malt flavorings and carbonated water.

plank: The central issue or issues of a political party or organization.

playbill: A poster announcing a theatrical performance.

premonition: A feeling that something is about to happen or will happen in the future.

quota: A fixed minimum or maximum number of a particular group of people needed for some activity, such as the number of soldiers needed for war.

ramrod: Rigid; stiff.

ratify: The act of formally approving something, such as a constitutional amendment.

rosette: An ornament made of material gathered together to resemble a rose, often worn as a badge or used as a decoration.

sarsaparilla: A sweetened carbonated beverage flavored with sassafras.

serendipity: Occurrence of an event by happy accident or finding valuable or agreeable things without trying to do so.

settee: A medium-size sofa with a back and arms.

shirtwaist: A woman's blouse or dress modeled on a man's shirt.

spinning mill: Factory in which fibers, such as cotton, are spun to produce thread for sewing or weaving.

sprocket: A wheel with tooth-like grooves that engage the links of a chain, as on a bicycle.

straw boater: A hat made out of stiff straw with a flat, rigid brim and top, often with a ribbon around the crown.

streetcar: A railcar that transported people within and between cities and towns on electric railways. See *interurban*.

strident: A harsh, insistent sound.

stubble: A rough surface of growth, such as of stalks or straw.

suffrage: The right of to vote. See *franchise*.

suffragette: A woman who advocates or publicly supports the right to vote for women.

suffragist: A person, man or woman, who supports extending the right to vote to those who are disenfranchised or do not have the right to vote.

telegram: A message sent by telegraph, via wire using coded signals.

telephone operator: A person who operates a telephone switchboard or otherwise provides assistance in establishing connections between people using landline telephones, especially on party lines.

temperance movement: The organized effort against the consumption of alcohol.

trench warfare: A type of combat in which opposing troops fight from trenches, or long narrow ditches, facing each other.

tsar: See *czar*.

u-boat: A German submarine.

valise: Suitcase.

vehemence: Intensity and insistence.

vociferously: Forcefully voicing an opposing viewpoint.

voyageur: A man employed by a fur company to transport goods between faraway places, especially during and after the American colonial era.

wanderlust: A strong longing or impulse to travel or wander.

Women's Franchise League: An English organization founded by Emmeline Pankhurst in 1889 to win the right to vote for women.

World War I: In Europe this war lasted from 1914 to 1918. The United States entered the war in 1917. At the time it was known as the war to end all wars and also as the Great War. Major players in this war were the Allies: Great Britain, France, Russia, and the United States vs. the Central Powers: Germany, Austria-Hungary, and the Ottoman Empire. The Allies won this war.

Selected Bibliography

Books

Cott, Nancy F. "Historical Perspectives: The Equal Rights Amendment Conflict in the 1920s." In *Conflicts in Feminism*, edited by Marianne Hirsch and Evelyn Fox Keller, 44–59. New York: Routledge, 1990. Available at Google Books.

Madison, James H., and Lee Ann Sandweiss. *Hoosiers and the American Story*. Indianapolis: Indiana Historical Society Press, 2014.

———. *Indiana through Tradition and Change: A History of the Hoosier State and Its People, 1920–1945*. Indianapolis: Indiana Historical Society, 1982.

Mill, John Stuart. "The Admission of Women to the Electoral Franchise, 20 May, 1867." In *The Collected Works of John Stuart Mill, Volume XXVIII—Public and Parliamentary Speeches, Part 1, November 1850–November 1860*, edited by Bruce L. Kinzer and John M. Robson. Toronto: University of Toronto Press, 1988.

Phillips, Clifton J. *Indiana in Transition: The Emergence of an Industrial Commonwealth, 1880–1920*. Indianapolis: Indiana Historical Bureau and Indiana Historical Society, 1968.

Newspapers

Abbs, Judith. "Ethel Smyth Belongs on the List of Great Women Composers." *Guardian Online*. http://www.theguardian.com.

"April is the Month of War." *Tippecanoe County Democrat*, Lafayette, Indiana, March 30, 1917. Available at NewspaperArchive.com.

"Denver Girls Will be Taught Marriage." *Lafayette Daily Courier*, Lafayette, Indiana, March 30, 1912. Indiana State Library Newspaper Division.

"First Women Appear on Jury in England." *New York Times*, July 29, 1920. Available at NYTimes.com.

Indianapolis Star, November 12, 1918. Available at NewspaperArchive.com.

"Just a Few Lines on Political Subjects." *Tippecanoe County Democrat*, Lafayette, Indiana, March 16, 1917. Available at NewspaperArchive.com.

Periodicals

Baer, M. Teresa. "World War I Letters to the Sammy Girls of Henry County, 1918–1919," *The Hoosier Genealogist: Connections* 41, no. 2 (June 2001): 101–6.

Cushman, Robert E. "Woman Suffrage Cases," *The American Political Science Review* 12, no. 1 (February 1918): 102–5. Available at JSTOR.org, doi:10.2307/1946347.

Fitzgerald, Gerard. "Chemical Warfare and Medical Response During World War I," *American Journal of Public Health* 98, no. 4 (April 2008): 611–25. Available at U.S. National Library of Medicine, National Institutes of Health, doi:10.2105/AJPH.2007.11930.

Marshall, Joan E. "The Changing Allegiances of Women Volunteers in the Progressive Era, Lafayette, Indiana, 1905–1920," *Indiana Magazine of History*, 96, no. 3 (September 2000): 251–85, http://www.indiana.edu/~imaghist/.

Ray, P. Orman. "Recent Primary and Election Laws," *American Political Science Review* 12, no. 2 (May 1919): 264–74. Available at JSTOR.org, doi:10.2307/1946203.

Resnick, Brian. "What America Looked Like: Collecting Peach Pits for WWI Gas Masks," *Atlantic Online* (February 1, 2012), http://www.theatlantic.com.

Documents

Abigail Adams to John Adams, March 31, 1776. Adams Family Papers: An Electronic Archive. Massachusetts Historical Society. http://www.masshist.org/digitaladams /archive/.

Anthems of the Suffragette Movement." How the Vote was Won. http://www.the suffragettes.org.

Gougar, Helen M. *The Constitutional Rights of the Women of Indiana. An Argument in the Superior Court of Tippecanoe County, Ind., Judge F. B. Everett, Presiding, January 10, 1895*. Typescript. Helen Gougar Collection, in Indiana Collection, G72c. Purdue University Libraries, Karnes Archives and Special Collections.

National Association Opposed to Woman Suffrage. "Some Reasons Why We Oppose Votes for Women." New York: 1894. Portfolio 130, Folder 13c. Library of Congress, American Memory. http://memory.loc.gov/ammem/index.html.

Nineteenth Amendment to the U.S. Constitution: Women's Right to Vote. *America's Historical Documents*. National Archives. http://www.archives.gov/historical-docs/.

"Teaching with Documents: The Zimmermann Telegram." U.S. National Archives. http://www.archives.gov/education/lessons/zimmermann/.

Wilson, Woodrow. "Wilson's War Message to Congress." Message to 65th Congress, 1st Session, Senate Document Number 5, Serial Number 7264, Washington, DC, April 2, 1917. Transcript. World War I Document Archive. https://wwi.lib.byu.edu /index.php/Wilson%27s_War_Message_to_Congress.

Zimmerman Telegram. *America's Historical Documents*. National Archives. http://www .archives.gov/historical-docs/.

Internet Sources

"75 Suffragists." Maryland Institute for Technology in the Humanities. http://mith .umd.edu/womensstudies/ReadingRoom/History/Vote/75-suffragists.html.

"1911–1916: Media Stunts for Suffrage." In "An Interactive Scrapbook of Elisabeth Freeman, Suffragette, Civil Rights Worker, and Militant Pacifist." http://elizabeth freeman.org.

"1914–1918: The Great War and the Shaping of the Twentieth Century." PBS. http:// www.pbs.org/greatwar/.

Ballard, Robert. "*Lusitania*." In "Lost Liners." PBS. http://www.pbs.org/lostliners/.

Borland, Elizabeth. "Music and Collective Identity in the Woman's Suffrage Movement." In "Women's Suffrage in the United States." College of New Jersey. http://www.tcnj.edu/~borland/2006-suffrage2/.

Boydston, Jeanne. "Women in the Labor Force." American National Biography Online. http://www.anb.org.

Cohen, Jennie. "The Mother Who Saved Suffrage: Passing the Nineteenth Amendment." History. http://www.history.com.

"Early History." National Woman's Christian Temperance Union. http://www.wctu.org.

"Elizabeth Cady Stanton." America's Story from America's Library. Library of Congress. http://www.americaslibrary.gov.

Ewing, Tom. "Influenza Precautions, Then and Now." Circulating Now. National Library of Medicine. http://circulatingnow.nlm.nih.gov.

Francis, Roberta W. "The History Behind the Equal Rights Amendment." Equal Rights Amendment. http://www.equalrightsamendment.org/.

"Great War and Jazz Age." America's Story from America's Library. Library of Congress. http://www.americaslibrary.gov.

Harper, Judith E. "Susan B. Anthony and Elizabeth Cady Stanton: Biography." *Not for Ourselves Alone*. PBS. http://www.pbs.org/stantonanthony/.

"Historical Timeline." Women's Basketball Hall of Fame. http://www.wbhof.com.

"History." League of Women Voters. http://lwv.org.

"Jeanette Rankin Casts Sole Vote Against WWII." History. http://www.history.com.

Kalvaitis, Jennifer M. "Indianapolis Women Working for the Right to Vote: The Forgotten Drama of 1917." MA thesis, Indiana University, 2013. Scholarworks. https://scholarworks.iupui.edu.

"Living Heritage: Women and the Vote." UK Parliament. http://www.parliament.uk/about/living-heritage/transformingsociety/electionsvoting/womenvote/.

"National Association Opposed to Woman Suffrage (NAOWS)." *Encyclopedia Britannica*. http://www.britannica.com.

National Nineteenth Amendment Society. "Carrie Chapman Catt: A Biography." Carrie Chapman Catt Girlhood Home. http://www.catt.org.

"Nellie Bly." *American Experience* on PBS. http://www.pbs.org/wgbh/americanexperience/.

"Nellie Bly." Bio. http://www.biography.com/.

"Patriotism or Equal Rights: The Suffragists Dichotomy during World War I." History Engine. University of Richmond. https://historyengine.richmond.edu.

"President Woodrow Wilson Speaks in Favor of Female Suffrage." History. http://www.history.com.

"Rankin, Jeannette, 1880–1973." History, Art, and Archives: United States House of Representatives. http://history.house.gov/people/listing/r/rankin,-jeannette-(R000055)/.

Rights for Women: The Suffrage Movement and Its Leaders. Online Exhibit. National Women's History Museum. https://www.nwhm.org.

"The Struggle for Democracy: Child Labour." In *Citizenship: A History of People, Rights, and Power in Britain*. Online Exhibition. UK National Archives. http://www.national archives.gov.uk/pathways/citizenship/.

"Tactics and Techniques of the National Woman's Party Suffrage Campaign." American Memory. Library of Congress. http://www.loc.gov/collections/static/women-of-protest/images/tactics.pdf.

"Topics in Chronicling America—World War I Armistice." Newspaper and Current Periodical Reading Room, Serial and Government Publications Division. Library of Congress. http://www.loc.gov.

United States Department of Health and Human Services. "The Great Pandemic: The United States in 1918–1919." Flu.gov. http://www.flu.gov/pandemic/history/1918/index.html.

United States Department of State. "U.S. Entry into World War I, 1917." In "Milestones: 1914–1920." Office of the Historian. https://history.state.gov/milestones.

"Women's Suffrage." In "Woodrow Wilson." *American Experience* on PBS. http://www.pbs.org/wgbh/americanexperience/.

"Woodrow Wilson." The White House. https://www._whitehouse.gov.

"World War I: Women and the War." Women in Military Service for America Memorial. http://www.womensmemorial.org.

"World War I and the American Red Cross." American Red Cross. http://www.redcross.org/mo3h.

"World War One: The Global Conflict that Defined a Century." iWonder. BBC. http://www.bbc.co.uk/iwonder.

The Wright Brothers and the Invention of the Aerial Age. Exhibitions. Smithsonian National Air and Space Museum. http://airandspace.si.edu/exhibitions/.

Subject Index by Chapter

Part 2: 1917